BEWARE!!
DO NOT READ THIS
BOOK FROM
BEGINNING TO END!

It's official: You're the Grand Prize Winner!

Pick your prize: a tour of the Hasley Toy Company, or Hasley's newest toy — a kid-sized robot called the Annihilator 3000. But choose carefully!

Take the tour and you'll get locked in the factory — where the toys come alive at night. Watch out for Zorgs. Those nasty monster toys want to suck out your brain. And stay away from Nasty Kathy. This living doll may look sweet, but her heart is pure evil!

If you choose the robot, make sure you're ready for trouble. The Annihilator is bent on destruction! First it goes after your cat. Then it goes after. . . *you*. Yikes! How do you disable a raging robot?

You're in control of this scary adventure. You decide what will happen. And how terrifying the scares will be!

Start on PAGE 1. Then follow the instructions at the bottom of each page. You make the choices.

SO TAKE A DEEP BREATH. CROSS YOUR FINGERS. AND TURN TO PAGE 1 NOW TO *GIVE YOURSELF GOOSEBUMPS*.

READER BEWARE —
YOU CHOOSE THE SCARE!

Look for more
GIVE YOURSELF GOOSEBUMPS adventures
from R.L. STINE

R.L. STINE

GIVE YOURSELF

Goosebumps®

TOY TERROR:
BATTERIES INCLUDED

AN
APPLE
PAPERBACK

SCHOLASTIC INC.
New York Toronto London Auckland
Sydney New Delhi Hong Kong

A PARACHUTE PRESS BOOK

ISBN-13: 978-0-590-93492-3

This edition is for sale in Indian subcontinent only.

First Scholastic Printing, August 1997
Reprinted by Scholastic India Pvt. Ltd., March 2008
January; August 2010; November 2011; January 2012;
July; December 2013; August; December 2014;
August; November 2015

Printed at Shivam Offset Press, New Delhi

"Hey, Mom! Look at this! I'm a winner!" you shout.

You race into the house with a letter that's just arrived in the mail. It came in a strange black envelope. Addressed to you. The words HASLEY TOY COMPANY are printed on the back.

"Look, Mom!" You wave the letter in the air. "I won!"

"That's nice." Your mother is reading the newspaper. She doesn't look up.

"Mom. For real! I won the Grand Prize!" you announce happily.

"That's great, sweetie." You can tell she's not really listening.

"I get my choice," you go on. "A tour of the Hasley Toy Factory, or their biggest and best toy — the Annihilator 3000. It's this totally cool robot. It's as big as I am!"

"The Annihilator what?" She looks up. You've got her attention now. "When did you enter this contest?" she asks.

Hey. That's weird, you think.

"I didn't," you admit.

Your mom looks concerned. "How did they get your name?" she wants to know.

Go on to PAGE 2.

You glance down at the envelope in your hand. It suddenly seems creepy that it's black.

"I don't know how they got my name," you admit.

Your mom thinks for a minute. "Maybe it was that electronic game we bought last year for your birthday. Remember? We sent your name in on the registration."

"That must be it," you say, sighing with relief. "Isn't it great that I won?"

"Oh, sweetheart." Your mom pats your shoulder. "Don't get your hopes up too high. Sometimes those contests are fakes. They say you've won, but then there's a catch: You have to buy magazines or something."

"No way!" you protest. "The letter doesn't say anything about magazines."

You hurry to the phone and call the special number in the letter. You dial it. A man answers. A man with a scratchy voice.

"Hello," he says, addressing you by name. "I've been waiting for your call."

Go on to PAGE 3.

"Which prize do you want?" the man asks.

You hadn't really thought about it yet.

And then it hits you. The man knew your name. But how?

A shiver goes down your spine.

You shake your head and try to concentrate. So he knew your name. Big deal. Not every kid on the planet has just won a huge prize!

"Hello? Are you still there?" the man calls.

You've got to say something. Which prize do you want? The letter says that if you take the tour of the Hasley Toy Factory, you'll get a free video game too.

But the Annihilator 3000 is the best toy the company makes!

"Uh, if I choose the tour of the toy factory, can I bring a friend?" you ask.

"Sure," he replies. "So what's it going to be?"

If you want to tour the Hasley Toy Factory, turn to PAGE 44.

If you want the Annihilator 3000, turn to PAGE 69.

4

You rush down the hall. The smiling robot stumps along behind you.

"How do I turn it off?" you shout to the good robot.

"Knock him over," the good robot advises. "There's a switch on the bottom of his feet."

You race to the kitchen and grab a broom. Then dash into the living room. The bad Annihilator is about to blast the couch!

You swing the broom hard. The robot tumbles over. You use the broom handle to flick off its switch.

"Hurray! I've hated him forever," the nice robot shouts. "Quick, throw him away."

You think about that for a minute. You're tempted. . . .

But what about when the class bully starts hanging around your yard? Trying to steal your bike? Or your lunch money?

You might *need* the bad robot someday.

Continue the story on PAGE 12.

On Monday morning, you and Officer Murphy, the toy policeman, arrive at your school for a special assembly.

When he is introduced, Officer Murphy glares sternly at the kids in the audience. "Children," he booms, "I'm here to show you some things that you should never do to your toys. Like this."

He tugs you to the front of the stage.

Then he pulls out a big black Magic Marker and scribbles all over your face!

"Hey!" you protest, spitting out ink. "Cut it out!"

"Or this," Officer Murphy continues as if you hadn't spoken.

He grabs you by the hair and drags you around the stage.

"Ow!" you yell. "Stop it! Ouch!"

"And never, *ever* let your pets get hold of your toys," Officer Murphy adds. "Like this!" He presses a remote control.

Barking furiously, Mittens, the mechanical Doberman, races across the stage and attacks your leg.

Hey — remember those crash test dummies they use to test cars? That's what you are now. So do the smart thing. Close the book.

And next time you read it, try not to be a dummy!

THE END

You stomp your foot on the ground.

No fair! you think, feeling totally disappointed. There's something going on in that factory. And now you'll never find out what it is.

A million questions spin through your brain.

They're good questions too.

But it's too late for all of them.

All except for one:

"What page do I turn to if I want to stay in the toy warehouse and find the doll?" you mutter out loud.

Uh-oh. Now you're talking to yourself.

But, okay. Since you asked, it's PAGE 76.

Now go on. You're out of the factory — so get out of this book. Because, as they say in showbiz:

THAT'S A WRAP!

You can't believe it. That doll was alive!

Your heart thumps with excitement.

You want to chase after her. You want to run over and tell Benny! You want to call a reporter and be interviewed on television!

But you decide to race home first — and get your dad's camcorder. If you can catch the doll on video, maybe you can sell it to the news. You could make a ton of money!

And besides — you figure no one will believe you about a living doll. Unless you get proof, that is.

You dash out the door of the factory and ride your bike home. Grab the camcorder. Stuff it in your backpack. Then pedal like crazy back to the factory.

When you return, Benny is waiting outside for you.

He has a horrified look on his face.

Turn to PAGE 32.

Seconds pass. And no laser blast.

You lift yourself onto your elbows and look back.

That flash wasn't the Annihilator. It was lightning.

You know, because through your kitchen window you can see the robot, still standing there.

You let out a sob of relief.

You scramble to your feet and run to Mrs. Carlyle's house. You yank open the door and stumble into the kitchen.

"Oh!" Mrs. Carlyle says, startled. "You scared me!" Then she sees your wet clothes and frowns.

"I'll get you a towel, dear," she says. As she bustles down the hall, she talks to you in a loud voice. "I was wondering when you'd come over. Your mom called a while ago. She said your phone isn't working. Must be the storm."

She comes back into the kitchen and drapes a towel over your shoulders. "Let me make you some hot chocolate," she clucks.

As Mrs. Carlyle busies herself at the stove, you peer through the window toward your house.

You see another blinding flash of light.

Then flames burst through your kitchen windows.

Your mouth drops open. You can't believe it.

Your house is on fire!

Turn to PAGE 14.

There must be a way you can fool the toys into thinking you're one of them. . . .

"Wait!" you cry as the soldiers dangle you over the belt. "You can't do this to me. I'm a toy too!"

Will they believe you? You're nearly choked with fear. The sound of the hair-planting machine makes your scalp crawl.

A few of the soldiers look uncertain. But the captain just laughs. "That's a lie," he declares. "Put the kid on the belt."

But some of the ninjas — the ones you saw making the robot police officer — rush in to help. One of them turns off the hair-planting machine.

"Maybe the kid is telling the truth. Maybe it's really a doll," another ninja warrior says.

"Ridiculous," the captain snaps. "Start up the machine."

The ninja hesitates, unsure. You gaze at him with pleading eyes.

"Please! Believe me," you plead. "I'm a toy."

"Prove it," the ninja replies. "Let's see your batteries."

Turn to PAGE 28.

You'd better call the toy company. Someone there can tell you how to stop this crazy robot.

"Hang in there, Patches!" you shout.

You race to the kitchen and pick up the phone.

But you don't know the number. You need the letter from the toy company. The one in the black envelope.

But it's on the desk in your room.

FZZZZZTTT!

Mrrrrrrroooooooowwwww!

Oh, no. Not again.

CLUNK, CLUNK, CLUNK.

The noise is right behind you.

You've got a bad feeling. . . .

You put the phone back on the hook, then turn around slowly.

Find out what's behind you on PAGE 122.

You and Benny creep through the warehouse toward the factory. Your eyes widen when you look through the glass wall.

The ninja action figures are out there, pulling switches and pushing buttons to run the machinery.

Then you see a figure standing still in the middle of the excitement. It's the doll you watched come to life!

Her brown hair is held in two pigtails with pink ribbons. Her little pink lips are heart shaped. She has huge blue eyes and rosy cheeks.

The doll lifts a megaphone to her lips.

"MOVE IT, YOU NO-GOOD NINJAS!" she roars.

You and Benny exchange startled glances. You look back and squint, trying to read the name stitched on her dress. Finally you make it out: NASTY KATHY. You've seen her on TV. Pull her string and she says all kinds of mean things.

"What are they making?" Benny whispers.

"More toys, I guess," you whisper back.

You both look at the conveyor belt. Then a bizarre cargo chugs into sight — a life-sized doll.

It looks so real, you'd swear it's alive. And lined up behind it are dozens more.

Turn to PAGE 40.

You decide to keep the bad Annihilator 1500 in your closet. Turned off. Just in case.

But you quickly throw the broken Annihilator 3000 in the trash. Along with the box it came in. You don't want your mom to know what happened.

She'd never believe it, for one thing.

And, besides, if she knew about the fires, she'd probably make you throw *all* the robots away!

Somehow, you'll have to do something about your dad's baseball cards. But you'll think about that another day.

A few minutes later, your mom walks into the house. The Annihilator 1500 is standing in the kitchen.

"Welcome home," the nice robot declares. "How may I serve you?"

Your mom takes one look at it and frowns. "I thought they were going to send you the Annihilator 3000," she says.

"Uh, well, they sent this instead," you reply.

Your mom shakes her head. "See? I told you not to get your hopes up too high. Those contests never turn out the way you hope they will. Just remember, Mom knows best!"

THE END

You and Benny glance at each other and shudder.

Evil toys are after you. They want to put you in the Dark Hole — whatever that is!

Murphy steps out of the car and stalks off. His hard shoes click along the road. They're the only sound in the night — other than the low hum of Bobaloo's car engine.

"Let's get out of here," Benny whispers.

"But if we go home, we have to ride our bikes the same way that — that *thing* — went," you object.

You eye Bobaloo's car.

The trunk is slightly open.

You start to get a crazy idea.

"Maybe we could sneak into Bobaloo's trunk and ride along with him," you say. "If we follow him, we might find out what's really going on."

Sounds risky, huh? Well?

How daring are you?

If you try to sneak past Officer Murphy and get home, turn to PAGE 54.

If you climb into Bobaloo's trunk, turn to PAGE 115.

14

You know that wasn't lightning.

It was the Annihilator. And it's burning down your house!

"No," you moan.

Then your stomach lurches. Patches! Patches is trapped in the house. If you don't rescue her, she'll burn up!

You race out into the wind and rain. Tree branches blow so hard, they whip your face.

"Patches!" you scream as you run. But the wind is roaring so loudly, you can barely hear your own voice.

Suddenly your ankle twists on a rock in the yard.

Your feet fly out from under you. The world turns over. And you land on your head. Hard.

"Ow," you moan.

Then everything around you goes black.

You're out cold. Wake up on PAGE 45.

You fall, banging your head on a shelf on the way down.

"Ouch. You stepped on my foot," a voice says in your ear.

Huh?

You gaze over and see the stuffed pig — the pig who talked to you when the toys first came to life. He's lying flat on the floor beside you, but he doesn't really seem hurt. He shakes himself off.

"Sorry I ran under your legs," he whispers. "But I had to stop you. To warn you. Don't go near the army. Nasty Kathy is there — and she'll get you! She's very, very mean."

"But I've got to help my friend," you explain.

Whoa! you think. This is too weird. You're talking to a stuffed animal. And it's talking back!

"There's only one way to save him," the pig whispers.

Just then Benny lets out a bloodcurdling scream.

You sit bolt upright.

"Don't go to him! Let him yell!" the pig advises. "Or neither of you will get out of here alive."

What will you do?

If you race to help Benny anyway, turn to PAGE 47.

If you take the pig's advice, turn to PAGE 74.

16

WHHHIRR ...

The Annihilator stares into the box for a minute. As if it's thinking. Wondering: Is this a trap?

Finally, it can't resist. Still whirring, it throws itself into the box headfirst. And starts ripping at your little brother's plastic toy.

Quickly you slam the flaps of the box closed, locking it in. You grab some heavy packaging tape. You stretch about sixteen pieces across the lid so it can't get out.

Then you phone the Hasley Toy Company and tell them to send a truck to pick up the Annihilator.

Turn to PAGE 31.

You're not usually clumsy. You decide to go left.

Forget the Hasley Toy Company, you think. I'm calling 911. . . .

You bolt. Running. Jumping. Dodging. Around the recycling bin. Over the newspapers. And through the dining room toward the living room.

RINNNGGGG!

Hey. The phone's ringing! That means it works!

You dash the last few feet to the living room and pick it up. Maybe it's your mom.

"Hello?"

"Hi!" comes the familiar voice of Becca Lester, a friend from school.

WHHHIRRR . . .

You can hear the Annihilator. But it's still in the kitchen. It hasn't made a move yet.

"Becca!" you pant. "I can't talk now."

But Becca doesn't listen. She just talks. That's Becca, for you. A real talker.

"You'll never believe what I heard about Jason Finestone," she tells you, launching into it.

"Becca. I *have* to hang up!" you tell her.

Just try *to hang up on Becca on PAGE 82!*

You hate the feeling of being trapped in the toy warehouse. Locked in. With that weird doll slinking around somewhere.

The whole thing gives you the creeps.

"Help!" you shout, pounding on the glass door. "Someone — let us out of here. Help!"

Nothing happens.

Silence.

Then suddenly Bobaloo steps out from behind some factory equipment. He's wearing a beret and carrying a megaphone.

He makes a disgusted face at you and starts shaking his head.

"Cut!" Bobaloo yells through a megaphone.

Cut? you think.

Cut what?

Find out on PAGE 64.

Your dad's oldest and most valuable baseball cards are in a shoe box on the desk. He's had them since he was a kid. They're worth a fortune.

He only let you borrow them because you promised to be extra-super-careful with them. You needed them for a school report.

A ray blasts out of the Annihilator's finger. Flames lick up the corner of the box.

"No!" you scream. "Stop it!"

This is insane. How do you turn this awful robot off?

You run around behind the Annihilator. You know its battery compartment is in its back.

Your fingers scrabble over the panel. Where's the latch? How do you open it?

The Annihilator spins around to face you.

How creepy! It's as if it could feel your touch.

Then it shoots a pale blue laser beam out of its chest — straight into your hand!

Turn to PAGE 25.

You and Benny hurry to the glass wall.

"She ran in here," you declare. "Into the warehouse."

"So what are we waiting for?" Benny asks sarcastically.

You notice that the glass door is open a crack. Jammed between the door and the frame is a tiny pink doll's shoe.

"Look! One of her shoes!" you shout, pushing open the door.

The two of you slip through. On the way in, Benny's foot bumps the shoe. The door shuts with a loud click.

You try to open the door. It won't budge.

"We're locked in," you announce.

"Who cares!" Benny cries. "Look at all these toys!"

Your eyes sweep over shelves of model cars, computer games, and hundreds of other toys. They all look so cool.

But you can't stop thinking about that doll.

She's in here somewhere. What is she up to?

Suddenly the thought of her gives you the creeps.

Do you really want to be locked in with her?

If you can't resist playing with the toys, turn to PAGE 76.

If you want to get out of the warehouse, pound on the door on PAGE 18.

You decide to grab the wheel of the car.

Hey! Wait a minute!

Do you have a driver's license?

Okay, how about a learner's permit?

Admit it. You're nowhere near old enough to drive, are you?

You can't drive — even *without* your hands taped together. But you're going to try it, anyway.

Okay. Go ahead and try it.

"Hey!" Bobaloo yells when you reach over him. For just an instant, he takes his eyes off the road.

Unfortunately, in that instant, the road curves around a sharp bend . . . and over a bridge. . . .

The road curves, but the car doesn't.

You, Bobaloo, and Benny go straight. Straight into a deep river at the bottom of a big hill.

Of course, Bobaloo and Benny are made of plastic — they *are* both toys — so they survive the crash. They're only a little banged up.

But, you . . .

Well, let's put it this way.

You just flunked your driving test!

THE END

This isn't happening, this isn't happening, this isn't happening! you tell yourself, squeezing your eyes shut.

You open your eyes.

You're still trapped between the hideous, slime-drooling Zorgs at your back — and the giant army in front!

The soldiers march toward you, aiming their weapons.

Then they fire!

Duck ... and try to stay down until you reach **PAGE 39.**

You lunge for the driver. Yank it out of the golf bag. Then grip it tightly in two hands.

SMACK! WHACK!

You swing the club down hard on the Annihilator's head.

A shattering, splintering noise fills the room.

CRA — ACCCCKKK!

The plastic body of the robot splits open. Right down the middle.

It cracks completely in two!

You shriek in horror when you see what's inside.

Face the horror on PAGE 38.

The entire warehouse is going to be crawling with living toys any minute!

You and Benny run to the end of the aisle just in time to see an army of remote-control cars zoom around the corner.

A squad of fifteen-inch-high ninja action figures climb out of their boxes and dart off.

Dolls. Robots. Dinosaurs. Soldiers. They pour off the shelves, laughing, snarling, shouting to each other.

Even the board games seem to be alive! One game has set itself up. The pieces are racing each other, and cards are flipping in the air.

"I don't believe this," Benny whispers.

Suddenly bright lights over in the factory flash on. They cast eerie shadows into the warehouse.

Then you hear a noise that makes your skin crawl. It's the sound of machines roaring to life. Conveyor belts whirring. Vats of plastic starting to bubble.

Someone — or something — is running the factory!

Hurry to PAGE 11.

"Yow!" you screech. The blue beam is freezing! You watch in terror as a block of ice forms around your right hand.

You dash down the hall to the kitchen. You smash your hand against the side of the sink. The ice shatters.

You turn on the hot water and let it run over your hand. You gasp and clench your teeth in pain.

This can't be happening, you think. It's a bad dream. Toys don't come to life and start burning your house down!

Burning! You remember your dad's baseball cards. The whole house will go up in flames if you don't get back there and put out the fire!

You grab a pitcher and shove it under the faucet. Then you race back to your room and hurl the water onto the box.

Whew! The fire is out. Dad's baseball cards are destroyed. But that's the least of your worries now.

Because the Annihilator isn't in your room anymore.

It's got to be somewhere in the house.

But, where?

Hurry to PAGE 113 before the robot does something worse!

Yikes! You'd better run before the Zorgs find you!

You quickly study the big map of the warehouse. Benny's voice sounded as if it came from Aisle Three. The dolls are in Aisle Two.

Your mind races. You know you should run to the doll aisle. You have to find Nasty Kathy's play trunk. That's where the pig said you'd find the key to turn off all the toys.

But what about Benny? He sounded like he was in big trouble. And the truth is, you're not sure you can hack this alone.

If you go straight to the doll aisle, turn to PAGE 42.

If you make a pit stop in Aisle Three, turn to PAGE 63.

"No way!" you shout at Nasty Kathy. "I may look like a doll, but I'm still human! I won't help you toys take over my world!"

You slide off the conveyor belt. Your doll body feels stiff and geeky. Your legs won't bend — they just swing like boards.

You run clumsily to a phone. With your plastic fingers, you frantically dial your house. When your mom answers, you quickly explain to her that you and Benny are trapped in the toy factory.

"Come get us — fast!" you tell her.

Your mom arrives with Benny's dad and two police officers. All the toys in the factory freeze. All except for you, that is.

"Mom!" you cry, jumping up and down. "Benny's tied up with jump ropes and they turned me into a toy!"

But instead of running to you, your mom starts screaming.

"What did you do with my child?" she cries.

"Don't worry, ma'am. We'll find the kid," one of the policemen says.

"We got a tip that there was something fishy going on with life-sized dolls in this factory," the other officer says. "Looks like this one is the leader."

Then the officers snap handcuffs onto your plastic wrists!

You have the right to turn to PAGE 70.

28

Prove it?

Your heart sinks. How can you prove you're a toy? You don't have any batteries.

But wait! Maybe you do have a chance after all.

Did you stop in Aisle Three before going to the doll aisle?

If you did, you'll have something tucked into the waistband of your jeans.

Something with a battery pack. . . .

Something you can use to fool the toys!

Well?

No cheating, now . . .

Because we'll catch you.

If you stopped in Aisle Three, you know what you picked up.

Is it a walkie-talkie? If so, turn to PAGE 81.

Is it a handheld video game? If so, turn to PAGE 125.

You can't see anything!

You touch the walls in the dark nervously. Your hand brushes a light switch. So you flip it on.

You squint in the light, glancing around the room. You're in some kind of basement office. There's a desk, a file cabinet, an empty shelf, and a phone.

A phone! you think. Yes!

You race over and lift the receiver to call the police.

Nothing. No dial tone.

The phone is dead.

In frustration, you slam the receiver down.

"How am I going to get out of here?" you moan.

A rustling noise on the shelf startles you. You glance up and see a dusty old toy clown in a red polka-dot suit.

"Hi," he says with a shy smile. "Want to play?"

"No," you answer desperately. "Stay away from me! I'm just trying to use the phone!"

"Oh." The clown shrugs. "That phone doesn't work. But you could use our phone if you want."

Try the clown's phone on PAGE 62.

In the next instant, the new Annihilator blasts the locks on the door and bursts into your living room.

You've got a robot behind you. And one in front.

Now you know how the filling in an Oreo feels.

WHIRRRR ... The new Annihilator lurches toward you.

Whittle steps through the door behind it. In a flash of lightning, the scar on his cheek shines white.

Terrified, you leap toward the fireplace and grab the first thing you can reach. A long, metal poker.

"Get away from me! All of you!" you shout. You lift the poker and start to swing it wildly.

The new Annihilator sends out a laser beam. It makes a horrible sizzling sound — as it whizzes right past your face!

Turn to PAGE 94.

By the time your mom gets home for dinner, the whole horrible mess is over.

Except for one thing.

Geoffrey's favorite toy is missing.

Uh-oh. You thought the Annihilator was trouble?

Wait till you see what Geoffrey can do!

THE END

Benny's eyes are wide with shock. "Where did you go?" he demands. "I can't believe you left. You missed the tour!"

"What?" you gasp.

"It's over," Benny says. "Boy, was it cool too. You wouldn't believe all the great video games they let me play."

"Oh, no," you moan. "It can't be over. I saw a doll come to life in there! We've got to get back in!"

You lunge at the factory door and yank on the handle. But it doesn't budge.

"It's locked," Benny declares behind you. "Give up. They all went home. The factory is closed."

It's true.

And, anyway, the batteries in your camcorder are dead!

So, hey — face it. It's time to recharge your batteries, rewind to PAGE 1, and start this book over.

Because for now, you have come to

THE END!

You've got to save your friend!

"Hang on! I'm coming!" you call, racing toward the sound of Benny's voice.

You zoom to the end of the empty aisle, then turn the corner and skid to a stop. The floor is covered with tiny plastic people — each one no taller than two inches. They're having a tea party. They gaze up at you with innocent eyes as you leap over them.

"Watch out!" one screams when your foot almost flattens it.

"Sorry," you say. You dance around, trying to keep from stomping on them. Just as you take another awkward step, you feel something squish under your foot.

Oh, no, I've killed it! you think.

Then you feel yourself slipping.

"*Ahhhhh!*" you cry as you crash to the cement floor.

Turn to PAGE 15.

You set the tank down and run to the burning bed.

You snatch a pillow and begin to beat out the flames.

SMACK! SMACK! The fire is going out, thank goodness.

You barely notice the Annihilator spinning away from you, turning toward your desk.

WHIRRRRRR ...

Until you see it raise its arm again.

"No!" you cry when you see where it's pointing. "Not my dad's baseball card collection!"

Turn to PAGE 19.

Benny turns over with a start. "It's you!" he says. "I thought you were those horrible soldiers for a minute. Cut me loose!"

"Sorry, Benny. I can't take the time," you apologize, rushing off toward Aisle One. "There's something else I've got to do first!"

You race to Aisle One, the learning toys aisle.

That's what the pig meant, isn't it? That you should go there?

But now what?

Now what do you do with the key?

Well . . . that depends.

Which key do you have?

If you have the silver key to Nasty Kathy's trunk, turn to PAGE 96.

If you found a different key inside the trunk, turn to PAGE 121.

You swallow hard.

What should you give the Annihilator next? More of your little brother's toys?

Yeah. Maybe.

WHHHIRRR ...

It's walking out of the kitchen.

You have to decide.

Are you going to try to figure out what it wants?

Or should you try to trick it back into its box?

If you still want to trick the Annihilator, turn to PAGE 59.

If you'd rather get it back into its box, turn to PAGE 88.

Benny screams as you try to leap away. Too late! The dog's sharp teeth clamp onto your pant leg.

You jerk away. But the dog is a big, fierce Doberman. And it won't let go.

"Benny! Help!" you cry.

Before Benny can move, a man with curly blond hair and black glasses races toward you.

"Mittens! Mittens, stop!" the man yells. He aims a remote control at the dog and presses a button.

The dog freezes in place. "These new models never work right," the man mutters as you yank your pants free.

Benny bursts out laughing. "Ha! It was just a toy!"

Your heart is still pumping a mile a minute. But you don't want to seem like a wimp. So you laugh too.

"Sorry about that," the man says. "I'm Bob Marvin, chief of new designs here at Hasley Toys — but everyone calls me Bobaloo. You must be here for the tour."

"Uh, yeah." You glance over at the motionless dog. Saliva still drips from its mouth, which is frozen in a snarl.

It looks so real!

This place is cool, you decide. You can't wait to see what's inside!

Follow Bobaloo to PAGE 55.

38

The shattered halves of the robot's body fall away.

WHIRRRR ...

WHIRRRR ...

There, in the wreckage, are two smaller robots. Two Annihilator 1500s!

They each look exactly like the Annihilator 3000. But half its size.

They roll forward, blinking their little lights and beeping. They seem to move much faster than the Annihilator 3000.

Then you notice. One of them has a smile on its face. And one has a frown.

"Hel-lo," the smiling one says in an electronic robot voice. "I am ready to serve you."

"Destroy. Destroy," the mean-looking one says as it rolls from the room.

On the way out, it shoots a laser beam. A pile of papers on your dad's desk *whoosh* into flames.

This one is even more powerful than the big Annihilator, you realize with horror.

You douse the fire with a pitcher of drinking water on the desk. Then you take off after the bad robot.

Catch up with the bad robot on PAGE 4.

"Nooooo!" you cry as the soldiers fire their weapons. You squeeze your eyes shut.

SSSSSTTTTTTT!

An instant later, you feel something sticky falling on your face. Your hair. Your arms and legs.

Yuck! They're squirting you with cans of Instant Spiderweb! The gooey threads cover you — trapping you in a tight net.

You struggle to move. To run.

But your arms are pinned to your sides by stringy spiderwebs. Your legs are trapped too.

"Help!" you cry, hoping Benny can hear you. "They've got me, Benny! They've got me!"

CLOMP-CLOMP-CLOMP. The soldiers' boots stomp the floor as they march up to take you prisoner.

They hoist you onto their shoulders. Eight soldiers on each side. Then they carry you into the factory — where Nasty Kathy is waiting. She looks angrier than ever.

"Good work," she tells the soldiers. "Now let's show this kid how it feels to be treated like a toy!"

Turn to PAGE 48.

Nasty Kathy barks orders into her megaphone.

"Keep moving, barf bags! You with the ugly face! Start loading the batteries."

One of the ninjas springs onto the conveyor belt. It opens a compartment in the foot of the first life-sized doll. It drops in several batteries, then clicks the compartment shut.

"Put a police uniform on it," Nasty Kathy snaps to another ninja. "And then turn it on."

A minute later, the big doll stands up and shakes itself.

It looks completely and chillingly human.

It snaps a salute at Nasty Kathy. "Officer Murphy reporting for duty, ma'am."

"Never mind that," Nasty Kathy growls. "Get out there and do the job you've been programmed to do."

"Yes, ma'am," the policeman replies. "But, first, what shall I do about the security problem?"

"Security problem?" Nasty Kathy snaps. "What security problem?"

The officer turns slowly until it's facing the glass wall you're crouched behind. Then it lifts its hand and points — directly at you!

Turn to PAGE 71.

The instructions will help you stop this maniac toy, you decide. You'll just reach over and try to pick them up.

WHIRRRRRRR...

The Annihilator is still watching you. Still waiting.

You crouch down slowly. You reach out. Grasp the piece of paper between two fingers. Pry it open and tilt it so you can read it without making any sudden moves.

WHIRRRRRR...

Your heart sinks. It's not the instructions at all. It's a note from your mom!

> *Hi, Kiddo,*
> *Gone to pick up Geoffrey at day care. But weather channel said there might be a hurricane — could trap me on other side of town. If I'm not home by 5:15, go next door to Mrs. Carlyle's. I'll call you if I have a problem.*
> *Love, Mom*

You gulp.

A hurricane? Things just went from bad to worse.

You glance out the window. The sky is growing dark. It's after five o'clock now. Maybe your mom is trying to call.

But she can't. The phone is dead!

Turn to PAGE 86.

You decide to go straight to the doll aisle and search for the key. The sooner you turn off the toys, the better.

Let Benny scream, the pig said. Or neither of you will get out of here alive.

You run along the cement-block wall in back of the warehouse, then turn toward the dolls in Aisle Two.

"Attention all monsters and soldiers," Nasty Kathy's voice booms over her megaphone. "Attack human scum in Aisle Two!"

A chill runs up the back of your neck.

How does she keep finding you?

SQUISH. FLAP.

You hear your least favorite sound. The sound of the Zorgs' feet as they suck and release the floor.

You've got to hurry!

Quick. Look for the key on PAGE 73!

You decide to go ahead and stick the computer disk in IT'S TIM.

You've got to. The pig said you'd never get out of here alive if you didn't!

You cram the disk into the slot in the back of the Incredible Talking Spelling Thinking Intelligent Machine.

SFFFFFFZZTT!

A flash of white-hot light nearly blinds you.

Then you hear a terrible hum. A hum so loud, you feel your bones shake.

Then silence.

You open your eyes. And gasp.

All the toys are . . . dead! Or, really, they're just toys again. They're not moving. Or breathing. Or talking.

For a moment, it seems strange. You were getting used to them. And you were getting downright fond of that little pig.

Then you snap out of it. And run over to find Benny in the action toys aisle.

Hey. How come he's just lying there? Stiff?

"Benny?" you call as you race toward him. "It's safe now."

You gasp when you get close enough to see his feet.

Turn to PAGE 111.

44

"I'll take the tour," you tell the man.

"Fine," he says. He gives you an address. "Be here at four o'clock Saturday afternoon."

"Thanks!" you say. Then you add, "Hey, how did I win this prize, anyway?"

But the man doesn't answer. He's already hung up.

The next day, you call your friend Benny and invite him to come with you on the tour. Benny just moved into the neighborhood — you've only known him for a couple of weeks. But your best friend is grounded for the third time this year. So you've been hanging out with Benny. He's funny, and he'll try anything once.

"Tour the Hasley Toy Company?" Benny says. "Cool!"

At four o'clock on Saturday, the two of you jump off your bikes in front of the factory. On top of the big white building a sign trumpets: WORLD'S LARGEST TOY SELECTION.

You open the door and step into the lobby.

The first thing you see is teeth. Two rows of glistening, sharp fangs!

It's a snarling guard dog! And it's headed straight for you!

Leap out of the way on PAGE 37.

You open your eyes and blink.

Your mom is sitting by your bed. In your own room!

"Mom?" you squeak, surprised. "What day is it?"

Your mom leans forward. "Tuesday, honey," she says, stroking your forehead. "I kept you out of school. You have a concussion."

"But the storm — the Annihilator," you murmur, still feeling weak and strange. "The . . . the house was on fire. And Patches was going to burn up, and —"

Your mom frowns. "No, sweetheart," she reassures you. "You must be a little confused. Patches is fine. And lightning did strike the house, but it didn't do much damage. Except — I hate to tell you this, sweetie — that toy you won . . . it burned up. We found it in the kitchen, all charred and ruined."

What a relief!

"But don't worry," your mom goes on. "I called the Hasley Toy Company, and they're sending another one."

"Oh, no!" you groan.

You'd like to close your eyes. But you know you'd better keep them open from now on. Because there's one thing you know about the Annihilator.

It will be back!

THE END

You dash into the living room. Patches is on the mantel over the fireplace. Her back is arched. The hair along her spine is standing straight up.

The Annihilator has her trapped! It zaps laser beams at her, but she keeps leaping out of the way.

Sparks flash against the stone chimney behind her.

"No more!" you scream. This robot has gone too far! Freezing your hand was bad. Burning up your father's fortune in baseball cards was worse.

But trying to blow up Patches — well, *now* it's personal.

You're still scared — but you're angry too.

You're going to send that toy back where it came from.

But how?

If you call the Hasley Toy Company, turn to PAGE 10.

If you try to trick the Annihilator back into its box, turn to PAGE 88.

You've got to help Benny! you decide. You can't desert your friend.

So you jump to your feet and start to run.

But as you round the corner, you trip again!

This time you're running so fast that you literally fly through the air. You've got plenty of time to look down and see where you're about to land.

In fact, time seems to pass in slow motion as you notice the sea of little green plastic army men below you. The kind you used to play with when you were younger.

There are *hundreds* of them. Each holding a little green plastic rifle. Tipped with a little green *metal* bayonet.

Pointing straight up at you.

Uh-oh. Those things look sharp!

Looks like you're stuck!

THE END

You squirm and wriggle, trying to free yourself. But the Instant Spiderweb is strong. You can't break through it.

"You look like a big, fat bug," Nasty Kathy sneers. "Too bad I already had my dinner."

Then she points to the conveyor belt — the one where you saw the life-sized dolls being made.

"Put the human scum up there," she orders the soldiers.

"Wait! No!" you cry. But everyone ignores you.

"Let's put our guest through the hair-planting machine!" Nasty Kathy squeals. "The one that punched holes in my scalp to put hair in my head. Let's see how a human likes that!"

"No!" you scream again. "Don't do it!"

THWACK. KA-CHUNK! You hear the horrible machine start up. Nasty Kathy cackles and hurries away.

As the soldiers start to lift you onto the conveyor belt, your mind races. Isn't there some way to escape these toys?

Maybe you could pretend to be a toy yourself. That police officer doll looked exactly like a person.

Or maybe you could try a bribe. . . .

If you pretend to be a toy, turn to PAGE 9.

If you try to buy your way out of this hairy situation, turn to PAGE 134.

The new robot suddenly opens its chest panel. A ball of electricity boils and glows inside. Then the ball shoots through the air — straight at the other robot!

Blue fire surrounds the old Annihilator. Sparks race up and down its body. Then it crashes over on its side. The lights fade from its eyes. The *whirring* noises stop.

Whittle lets out a sigh of relief.

"Sorry about that," he apologizes. "But somehow when we shipped you your prize, we sent you the wrong model. That was a new test version of the Annihilator 3000. I've been trying to give it a brain. But, so far, no luck."

"You — it —" you stammer. You don't know what to say!

"I knew you were in trouble when I got the robot's E-mail message," Whittle continues. "Hope it didn't do too much damage before I came."

"Damage?" You think of the fires. Your cat. "Actually —"

"Never mind about that," Whittle interrupts. "I'm sure it was worth it. Especially since now we'll put your name in the big drawing. You have a chance to win our Super-Extra-Special Grand Prize . . . the Annihilator 4000!"

The Annihilator *4000*? Oh, no!

Better get a fire hose ready!

THE END

50

The best way to help Benny is to get out of the factory and bring back some grownups, you decide. There's no way you can fight off Nasty Kathy's army alone.

You tiptoe toward the red light.

Benny's screams float . down the aisle. "*Oooooh* — they're hurting me!"

"Sorry, Benny," you mutter. It feels bad to leave your friend. But if you stay, you're both finished!

As you approach the red light, your heart sinks.

It's not an exit sign.

It's just a dumb red light coming from a stupid metal box.

You've backed yourself into a corner — and there's no door!

Your heart starts to pound. How will you get away when all those creepy toys catch up to you?

Try to back out on PAGE 133.

What is the robot thinking? you wonder. What does it want?

It's hard to tell. But if the Annihilator is as alive as it seems to be, maybe there's some way to trick it.

It's worth a try, anyway.

Your heart pounds as you scan the kitchen. Searching for something good to offer the robot.

What would it like? you ask yourself. A cookie? A glass of milk? Somehow the Annihilator doesn't seem like the milk-and-cookies type.

Then you spot your little brother's toy fire truck under the kitchen table. It's a dumb baby toy. But it does light up and make sounds. Kind of like the Annihilator — but not as bad tempered.

You pick up the fire truck and hold it out to the robot.

The robot raises an arm. Its eyes glow brighter. Then it takes the truck from you!

See what happens next on PAGE 79.

You grab the tank. Water sloshes onto your sneakers.

You look into the tank and see your guppies — Simeon and Seth — flitting around. Opening and closing their little mouths. They're as frightened as you are!

You can't kill Simeon and Seth!

Put the tank down and go to PAGE 34.

If you go with Nasty Kathy, you'll never find the key to turn off the toys. And you'll never get out of the factory alive!

You hesitate, pretending to think about it.

"Come on!" Nasty Kathy bellows. "We don't have all night!" She drops the tip of her Laser Blaster just an inch.

It's the chance you were waiting for.

"No!" you shout, giving her a shove. Then you take off running in the opposite direction.

You hear a whine from the Laser Blaster. A red beam sizzles past your head. But you don't look back. You make it safely down to the end of the preschool toys aisle. Back to the big overhead sign listing all the toys in the warehouse.

"Yo! Human moron!" Nasty Kathy calls over her megaphone. "You'll never get away!"

You're sweating, and your breathing is heavy. But you can still hear her footsteps as she runs down the next aisle.

Then you hear her on the megaphone again.

"Attention all Zorgs. Report to Aisle Four. Dinnertime!"

Aisle Four?

That's where you are!

Turn to PAGE 26.

"Let's try to make it home," you whisper to Benny.

Benny frowns. "Okay, but I'm really tired," he says slowly. "I hope I can pedal my bike."

You eye Benny suspiciously. That's a weird thing to say, considering you're both being chased by living toys.

But after all, it has been quite a day.

You and Benny wait quietly until Bobaloo pulls away. Then you hop on your bikes and pedal slowly toward town.

When you approach the gas station, you see the owner, Willy Sanderson. He's talking to Officer Murphy!

They're standing under a streetlight. A police patrol car is parked nearby.

You don't want to be seen. But you have to know what they're saying. You and Benny wheel your bikes behind a bush and creep close enough to hear them.

"How many of us are there?" Murphy asks quietly.

"Oh, at least fifty," Sanderson answers. "I've lost count."

You gasp. Fifty toys pretending to be humans?

Who are these dolls? Are any of them people you know?

Turn to PAGE 60.

Bobaloo swipes a magnetic key card over a panel and pulls open another door. The three of you walk into the huge factory.

The room is full of chugging machinery and whirring conveyor belts. Wow, you think, gazing around. This is awesome!

Across the factory is a huge glass wall. Through the glass you can see a warehouse. Its shelves are stacked to the ceiling with toys.

"This way," Bobaloo calls, pointing toward the warehouse. He and Benny hurry off.

You start to follow them — when something catches your eye. Something you can hardly believe.

A line of dolls in pink dresses are riding on a conveyor belt. One of them suddenly sits up — and looks around.

For one second, her big blue eyes glance your way. She flutters her long lashes in surprise. Then she jumps off the assembly line and darts behind a machine.

Whoa. Did you really just see a *living* doll?

You rub your eyes and blink hard. Should you run after it?

Or should you run home and get your dad's camcorder?

If you run after the doll, turn to PAGE 98.
If you go for the camcorder, turn to PAGE 7.

"We toys are on a mission," Nasty Kathy explains. "A mission to stamp out toy abuse!"

"Huh?" You stare at her. "You mean you're not going to take over the world?"

Nasty Kathy snorts. "Don't be dumb! What would we do that for? No, we just want to make the world a little better for toys. To stop kids from ripping the eyes off their teddy bears, pulling off their dolls' heads, stuff like that. That's why we're making all the police dolls. Someone has to control these kids!"

"Oh . . ." you murmur, and trail off.

You feel kind of let down. You were expecting to hear something more exciting. Something more adventurous.

But you promised to help out. "Count me in," you declare. "What do you want me to do?"

Nasty Kathy grins, showing her pointed teeth.

You shiver. Even though you're on *her* side now, she's still kind of scary.

"You're going to be our demonstration doll!" she announces.

Start your new job on PAGE 5.

You and Benny dash across the runway toward the plane. You hide behind a luggage cart. While Bobaloo talks to the pilot, you slink up the stairs. Then you hide behind some seats in the back of the small plane.

Finally Bobaloo and two other men get on board. The pilot radios to the tower, taxis down the runway, and . . . you're flying!

"Where to?" you hear one of the men say.

"First stop — Walt Disney World," Bobaloo replies.

"Cool!" Benny blurts out.

"Hey — who's back there?" a man with a gruff voice asks.

He stomps to the back of the plane. You see his big feet through the metal chair legs. Is he a huge toy? you wonder.

You try to crouch lower, but he can see you easily.

"Looky what we got," the man calls to Bobaloo. "Stowaways!"

Bobaloo hurries back.

"This must be my lucky day," he says, staring at you coldly.

Find out what Bobaloo's idea of a lucky day is on PAGE 120.

"Aaahhhhhh!" you scream as the monsters fly at you.

All six Zorgs latch on to your legs and claw their way up your body toward your face!

You thrash wildly and manage to shake two of them loose. They land with a plop near your feet.

But the ones that hang on grip tighter.

RIIIIIPPPPPP! Their razor claws slice through your jeans as they climb. You feel the sting of the ooze from their tongues as it drools into the scratches in your flesh.

"HEELLLLP!" you scream. They're spitting slime!

You grab at them with your hands, but they're strong. Hard to shake off. You gaze down and shudder. Their filthy blue-green fur ripples. Their slimy tongues waggle. Their ugly sucking feet grip your legs.

Two more monsters leap again. Harder. Higher. Their claws sink into your T-shirt. You grab one and hurl it across the room.

Then you feel a claw scrape along your chin. . . .

Go on to PAGE 67.

Your plan is to try to trick the Annihilator. It's the only way you can control it.

At least, that is your plan — until you follow the robot into your dad's office.

Its eyes light up when it sees your dad's new laptop computer. It holds out a hand again.

You gulp and shake your head. The Annihilator is scary.

But so is your dad when he's miffed!

"No way," you say. "You can't have the computer. My dad is already going to kill me about the baseball cards!"

The Annihilator spins toward you and raises its arm.

ZZTT! A laser beam shoots out.

"Ouch!" you cry, jerking your hand away from the shock.

The Annihilator whirls back toward the computer and flashes its lights again. The message is clear. It wants the computer.

Forget controlling the robot. You have to disable it for good! You scan the office frantically for some kind of weapon.

Then your eyes light on your dad's golf clubs. His new metal driver twinkles in the light.

Should you try to tee off on the robot's head?

If you give the robot the computer, turn to PAGE 110.

If you smack it with a golf club instead, go to PAGE 23.

Fifty fake humans. Living in your town. They look so real — you could never tell.

Then you remember the ninja popping batteries into Officer Murphy's foot. Hey! That's the way to tell if someone is really a toy! By looking at his feet!

Officer Murphy starts walking toward the squad car. You and Benny creep toward your bikes. You've got to tell someone about this plan — once you know who you can trust.

Just then you accidentally kick a rusty can lying in the grass. It rattles onto the road. Noisily.

"Who's there?" Murphy shouts.

You start to run. Murphy sprints after you like lightning. He grabs you by the shirt and hoists you up in the air.

"Let go!" Benny shouts. In a flash, your friend leaps on the officer and somehow pries his hand loose!

The plastic policeman quickly turns and grabs Benny, instead.

"Run!" Benny shouts at you. "Go on — run!"

"What about you?" you cry as the officer drags Benny away.

"I'll be okay!" Benny shouts. "Just run!"

Poor Benny, you think. He's history! And he saved your life.

But you do run. Like crazy.

Run to PAGE 119.

You make a break for it — running to the right.
Right past the Annihilator . . .
Oops!
Tripped already, did you?
Whoa! And hit your head on the way down too.
Well — you said you were clumsy!
"Ahhhh!" you cry. Your arms flail as you reach for something to break your fall.
Uh-oh. You shouldn't have grabbed *that*.

Find out what you grabbed on PAGE 99.

You stare at the phone the clown is pointing to. It's a blue plastic toy phone at the back of the shelf. A baby toy.

Hey, you think. All the toys are alive. So maybe — just maybe . . .

You lift the blue plastic receiver to your ear.

HUMMMMM. A dial tone! Yes!

Your heart beats a little faster as you push 911.

"What is your emergency?" a woman's voice answers.

Yes! You're going to make it out of here after all.

"It sounds crazy," you say, swallowing hard, "but I'm trapped in the Hasley Toy Factory. The toys have come to life! They're using the machinery to make human beings or something!"

You clear your throat, waiting for the policewoman to laugh or hang up. But she doesn't.

"Okay," she replies quickly. "Don't worry. We'll get someone over there on the double."

"Thanks." You hang up and start to thank the clown.

But the door behind you slams open. Before you can turn around, someone taps you on the leg.

"Don't move," a deep voice orders. "You're under arrest!"

See who's behind you on PAGE 92.

You zoom around the corner and head into Aisle Three.

It's crowded with toys, open boxes, and assorted junk.

With the dim emergency lights barely glowing overhead, you can't really see what's going on.

You squint. It looks as if the toys have set up a barricade.

What is that large lump at the end of the aisle? That thing lying on the floor, near the glass wall. . . .

Oh, man. You've just figured it out.

"Benny!" you shout.

Benny is tied up with about a dozen jump ropes. He looks like a giant lying on his back, with dozens of tiny soldiers standing on his chest.

"Help me!" he shouts. "Hurry! They're crawling all over me!"

You run toward Benny.

Then you hear the sound you've been expecting . . . and dreading!

SQUISH. FLAP. SQUISH. FLAP.

Rush to PAGE 91.

64

One by one, six other people step out from various hiding places in the factory.

One man has a movie camera resting on his shoulder. A woman carries lights and a microphone on long poles.

It's a movie crew! you realize.

Bobaloo hurries to the glass door and lets you out.

"All right, all right," he says. "Don't bawl. We weren't going to leave you in there all night or anything!"

He signals to the rest of the crew.

"Never mind," he says over the megaphone. "This one didn't work out. Let's wrap it up. We'll try again next weekend."

"Wrap what up?" you ask. "What's going on?"

"We're shooting a commercial here," Bobaloo explains. "You know — catch the excitement of a kid locked in a toy factory. Your friend Benny, here, has the right spirit. But you didn't act excited. You acted terrified. So you're out — and he's in. Thanks for coming." He ushers you to the door.

"Wait!" you cry. "What about the doll I saw come to life? And how did you get my name, anyway?"

But it's too late for those kinds of questions. Bobaloo kicks you out of the factory and slams the door.

Turn to PAGE 6.

You hold the disk tightly in your fist. Which aisle were the learning toys in? You close your eyes and try to picture the big overhead sign.

Uh-oh. Big mistake. You never should have closed your eyes.

By the time you open them again, you're surrounded!

There are Zorgs on the floor at your feet. And beside you, they're hanging from the shelves — reaching for you. Flexing their claws. Licking their lips.

"No!" you cry out.

Half a dozen of them leap onto you in a flurry of foul-smelling fur.

You swing your arms like windmills, flinging two monsters off your shirt. Then you start to run toward the glass wall.

But, marching in formation down the doll aisle, blocking your way, is a squad of big wooden soldiers.

How are you going to get out of this one?

Turn to PAGE 22.

The phone slips from your hand. It hits the floor with a clunk.

The Annihilator watches you.

Motionless.

Waiting for you to make the next move.

Your gaze darts frantically around the kitchen. Then, out of the corner of your eye, you spot a folded piece of paper. . . .

Maybe it's the instruction sheet! The one that came in the box with the Annihilator!

Suddenly you're dying to read those instructions. They could tell you how to turn the crazy robot off.

WHHHIRR . . .

The Annihilator takes a step toward you. Then stands motionless again.

Are you going to reach for the instructions?

Or should you make a run for it? Maybe the phone in the living room is still working. . . .

If you reach for the instructions, turn to PAGE 41.

If you try to dash to another phone, turn to PAGE 75.

"NOOO!" you cry. You kick and punch at the monsters. Finally all six of them drop to the floor.

Then you turn and run. But you have to dodge some remote-control cars that are zooming in wild patterns at your feet.

The cars are trying to trip you!

A plastic tea set hurls itself off a high shelf. Cups and saucers clatter down on your head.

All the toys are out to get me! you realize.

You hop over a slithering rubber snake. On the wall ahead, you see a sign listing all the toys: CARS & TRUCKS. LEARNING TOYS. ACTION FIGURES. STUFFED ANIMALS. PRESCHOOL TOYS. Under it is a map of the aisles.

Which way is it safe to go?

You bend down and peer between the empty shelves. . . .

Hey. Is that a glowing red light in the back corner of the warehouse? The kind they use on exit signs?

You start to crawl toward the red light.

Then you hear Benny's voice. Far away. Desperate.

"Help," Benny cries. "Help! They've got me!"

If you follow the sound of Benny's voice, turn to PAGE 33.

If you go toward the red exit light, turn to PAGE 50.

You decide to listen to your friend.

He sounds so certain. And so desperate!

You hurry to the aisle where Benny is tied up.

"Untie me," he shouts. "Just do as I say."

You untie the jump ropes that hold him down. As soon as he's free, he jumps to his feet.

"What's going on?" you ask. "How did you know —"

"No time for that now. Just listen to me."

Benny seems so different. So in control.

He continues, "Run to Aisle One and get IT'S TIM. Bring it with you — no matter what. Then we've got to grab some more good stuff. I'll get the computer games, a Laser Blaster, the hockey game, and a remote-control car. You get whatever toys you want. Then run for your life and meet me at the front door."

Your eyes widen. "What if I run into Nasty Kathy?"

"Just go!" Benny answers.

Do what Benny says on PAGE 107.

You have to have the Annihilator.

It looks *so* cool on TV. It's as tall as you. It's black and purple. With eyes that light up and lasers in its hands. It walks. It runs. The TV commercials say the Annihilator is "totally bent on destruction."

It even comes with a set of little spacemen — which it can destroy. Then you can put the spacemen back together.

Best of all, you can program the Annihilator to do just about anything. "Anything except your homework!" the ad says.

"I'll take the Annihilator 3000," you answer quickly.

"Great!" the man replies. "It's too late to get it to you tomorrow. But we'll deliver it on Monday. Got that?"

"Sure!" you declare. "Thanks!"

"My pleasure," the man answers with a strange chuckle. "Good-bye . . . and good luck."

"Wait!" you exclaim. "How did you know my name? How did I win this prize, anyway?"

But the telephone line has gone dead.

Turn to PAGE 77.

They put you under arrest for impersonating a human.

It's a serious crime. But because it's your first offense, the judge lets you off easy. Instead of going to jail, you just have to do community service.

Your sentence? Two months as the guest star on the *Dudley the Purple Dragon* TV show.

It's pretty embarrassing to be on the Dudley show. You even have to sing the stupid Dudley song. But after your two months are up, you stay on to make a little money. You're saving up so you can afford the expensive surgery to have your plastic doll shell removed.

Hey. They don't call them "plastic" surgeons for nothing, you know!

THE END

You've been spotted! You're so terrified, you can't move.

Nasty Kathy's head swivels in your direction. Then she grins. She has two rows of small, sharp teeth.

"*I'll* deal with them," Nasty Kathy tells the officer. "You go out there and do your job."

"Yes, ma'am," Officer Murphy says, striding off.

Nasty Kathy walks over to you. Without saying a word, she reaches up and pulls the string on her own back.

"I don't *like* you!" a tinny voice shrieks.

Nasty Kathy giggles. This time her mouth moves. "You shouldn't be here. Humans can't know about our plan. Now you're going to pay," she says.

"No, we're not!" Benny yells. "This tour was supposed to be free!"

He jumps up and dashes through the glass door into the factory. Tearing past a group of knee-high ninjas, he races toward the front door. Then he vanishes behind a big machine.

You start to follow him. But then you realize . . . that's the door the police officer doll used.

What if it's still out there?

Take your chances with the police doll on
PAGE 93.

If you'd rather find a different way out, race to
PAGE 123.

You lean over the robot's shoulder — and gasp when you see what's on the computer screen.

It's hooked up to the Internet! It's sending E-mail!

The message it's writing is addressed to Jim Whittle, chief toy designer at the Hasley Toy Company. It says:

> Whittle,
> I have arrived and taken control. Fire, terror, destruction. Only one person at home — a child. Don't worry — I will not allow it to leave the house. I await further instructions.
> Annihilator 3000

Almost instantly, a reply flashes across the screen:

> Annihilator,
> Stay there and do nothing. I am only a few blocks away. I will arrive shortly.
> Whittle

You race to the living room and peer out the window. The sky is still gray-black and stormy. Wind howls in the trees. Thunder and lightning pierce the blackness every few seconds.

But the storm is nothing compared to the jolt you feel when you see what's in front of your house.

Find out what's coming on PAGE 130.

Find Nasty Kathy's trunk! is all you can think. If you can only find that key, you can save Benny and yourself.

You trot down the aisle, scanning the shelves. Dolls are everywhere! Sitting on the shelves, chatting to each other, drinking from baby bottles. Two fashion dolls are lounging on recliners.

"Chip is coming over in his new sports car," you hear one say.

Finally you spot a navy blue and silver doll's trunk. NASTY KATHY is painted on the front.

A silver key dangles in the lock.

"Awesome!" you shout, pumping your fist in the air. "I found it!"

You reach up to take the key.

That's when you feel something that makes your blood run cold. Something small and strong . . . gripping your leg . . .

And starting to climb up your jeans!

Please don't let it be a Zorg! you think.

A Zorg or not a Zorg? That is the question. Find out the answer on PAGE 103.

"Okay," you agree nervously. "Tell me how to save him. But please hurry! It sounds like they're killing him!"

"You've got to find the key to turn us off," the pig says. "To turn off *all* the toys."

"Huh?" You stare at him, your mouth open.

Did the pig just say there's a way to turn off all the toys?

"Wait a minute," you reply. "Why are you trying to help me?"

"Because it's a nightmare here," the pig whispers. "Every night, the army starts fighting. The monsters stalk us. The cars and trucks roar up and down the aisles. It's very scary."

The pig sniffles and swipes at its eyes with its foot.

"And do you know what else?" it continues. "I don't like Nasty Kathy. Once she called me a putrid porkface."

You bite your lips, trying not to laugh.

"Laugh if you want," the pig declares. "But Nasty Kathy is very dangerous. She's got a secret plan."

Listen to the pig on PAGE 78.

You have to call 911. Or the toy factory. Or someone. Anyone!

You get ready to make a run for it. To another phone. The one in the living room.

Let it be working! you pray.

WHHHIRR ...

The Annihilator studies you coldly.

You swivel your head slowly, judging the best way to run.

If you go right, around the counter, you'll have a straight shot to the living room. But you'll have to pass inches from the Annihilator.

If you go left, you'll have to dodge the recycling bin and jump a stack of newspapers. It'll take some fancy footwork. But it seems safer. You'll stay farther from the robot.

And you'll probably make it ... if you're not too clumsy.

Well? Are you? Clumsy, that is? Be honest, now.

If you're usually clumsy, go to the right on PAGE 61.

If you're not usually clumsy, go left on PAGE 17.

Benny runs toward the video games.

A kid-sized red sports car catches your attention. You climb in. But before you can turn the key, all the lights in the warehouse shut off. And everything goes black!

"Hey!" Benny screams. "What's going on?"

You grope your way toward his voice. "Maybe the factory is closing," you suggest. "It's Saturday — and it's after five o'clock."

"So we're stuck in here for the rest of the weekend?" he whispers, sounding scared.

"No way. Bobaloo will come back for us," you declare.

Just then, dim emergency lights flicker on.

"Um, I forgot to tell you," Benny says. "Bobaloo got called away for some kind of emergency. He told me to find you and then — well, we were supposed to leave."

Oh, great! you think. Then you remember your other problem.

"That doll must still be in here with us," you whisper.

"Aw, you made that up," Benny says.

"No I didn't," you insist. "She was —"

You stop talking when you hear a thump. It's coming from a shelf above Benny's head. Was it that doll?

You brace yourself — and look up.

Turn to PAGE 118.

Weird, you think. He hung up so fast. And what did he mean by "good luck"?

Still, you can't wait for the Annihilator 3000 to arrive.

You rush in to tell your mom about the phone call.

She frowns. "Just don't get your hopes up," she says.

"Wait until Monday, Mom," you tell her. "You'll see."

"That reminds me," she says. "Monday afternoon I've got to pick up your brother, Geoffrey, at day care. I won't be here when you get home from school."

In your heart, you're afraid that your mom might be right. That the prize won't arrive.

But you rush home on Monday after school, hoping she's wrong. Hoping the package will be waiting. . . .

From the street, the porch looks empty.

Until you run up the front steps.

A huge brown cardboard box is sitting near the front door.

"Yes!" you cry the minute you spot it.

Open it on PAGE 84.

"What secret plan?" you ask, wide-eyed.

The pig glances around to make sure no one is listening.

"All I know is, they're making human-sized dolls in there," he whispers, nodding toward the factory. "They have some kind of a plan to change the world. But they won't tell us baby toys what it is. I don't trust them. So you've got to get the key and turn us off. It's the only way."

"All right." You nod solemnly. "But where's this key?"

The pig leans forward. You can feel his pink fur tickling your ear.

"She has it," he whispers so quietly, you can hardly hear him. "It's in Nasty Kathy's play trunk."

"Did someone call my name?" a nasty voice growls.

You whip your head around — and gasp.

It's Nasty Kathy. She's standing right behind you.

And she has a Laser Blaster in her hands!

Turn to PAGE 116.

The Annihilator studies the fire truck. Then it switches the toy on.

WHEEEEEEE! goes the truck's siren. The Annihilator seems to jump a little. Then it leans down and rolls the truck back and forth on the floor.

The Annihilator is playing! you think. All the lights on its face are pulsing brightly. It *whirs* excitedly.

Then the truck's siren peters out. Its lights go off.

Uh-oh. The batteries are dead!

Turn to PAGE 137.

"Thanks for your advice. But no thanks!" you yell at the hand on your shoulder.

You reach up and hurl it to the ground. It lands with a plop and then skitters under a shelf.

You pocket the silver key and race toward the glass wall at the end of the aisle.

The Zorgs are only a few steps behind you as you rocket around the corner into Aisle Two.

"Whoa!" you gasp when you see what's at the end of the doll aisle.

Soldiers. Dozens of them!

Except these aren't two inches tall and green.

They're big wooden soldiers! Nasty Kathy's size!

They're milling around, telling stupid jokes and comparing weapons. You slink rapidly down the aisle, next to the shelves. Hoping the soldiers don't look your way.

Turn to PAGE 22.

The walkie-talkie in your waistband! It has batteries. You could pretend they're yours. You're saved!

The problem is, how can you reach the walkie-talkie with your arms tied?

Meanwhile, one of the ninjas takes off your shoes and socks. He moves his little fingers around on the bottom of your feet. It tickles!

But you don't feel like laughing.

"The kid lied!" the ninja shouts. "There's nothing here but skin!"

"Wait!" you yell. "I *am* a toy! I keep my batteries in a different place. If you cut one of my arms free, I'll show you!"

"ENOUGH!" the army captain commands. "Shut the kid up!"

One of the soldiers aims a web-gun at you. It only takes one squirt. Right over your mouth. The sticky spiderweb spray oozes down your cheeks and silences you. You can barely breathe.

Nasty Kathy walks back over. She flips the ON switches for the conveyor belt and the hair-planting machine.

TWHACK. KA-CHUNK! THWACK KA-CHUNK!

Turn to PAGE 114. If you dare!

"So, anyway," she says, completely ignoring you. "Jason got sent to the principal again last week. And his parents were so mad, they decided to send him to military school! So he ran away from home, but he only went to the park, really. Then a squirrel bit him, and now he has to get rabies shots, so he can't go to military school for at least a month, and . . ."

WHIRR . . .

Oh, no. The Annihilator is here!

"Becca!" you cry desperately. "I'm hanging up n ——"

ZZZZTTTT! A blue laser beam zips out of the Annihilator's chest and works its way up your body, from your toes to your head.

Becca's voice goes on and on. And there's nothing you can do. You just stand there with the phone frozen to your ear. Really frozen. As in ten below zero.

Guess Becca's story about Jason left you cold!

THE END

"Benny!" you gasp. "What are *you* doing here?"

Benny gulps and gives you a nervous smile.

"Uh, hi," he blurts. "I came here looking for you. I figured you'd run to Amy's house."

"Come in," Amy calls. She steps around Benny, drags you into the living room, and quickly closes the door.

She peeks out the front window nervously. As if she's watching to be sure no one followed you. Or saw you come in.

"What's going on?" you ask. Your head spins with questions. Is Benny in on the toys' plot? And Amy?

"Nothing's going on," Amy tells you. "Benny just came to find you. That's all. What's the big deal?"

Your eyes narrow. You stare at Benny. "How did you get away from Officer Murphy so fast?"

"Oh, I told him that we were lost and didn't know how to get home," Benny declares. "He believed me."

Hmmm. You find that story kind of hard to swallow.

Especially since the phony policeman saw Benny hiding with you in the toy factory!

You wonder if you should believe a word Benny says. He is your friend — but you haven't known him very long.

If you believe Benny's story, turn to PAGE 101.
If you're suspicious of him, turn to PAGE 126.

The box is so heavy, you can't lift it.

You toss your jacket and backpack aside. Then you drag the box through the door and into the living room. You never imagined it would be so heavy!

Something *whirs* softly inside the sealed box.

Weird, you think. It sounds as if the Annihilator is already turned on. . . .

You're so excited, you rip the carton open.

WHIRRRR!

The motor inside the robot sounds like it's spinning.

You tilt the carton onto its side. Slide the heavy purple and black robot onto the living room rug.

You crawl halfway into the box, but all that's in there is the stupid instruction sheet. Who needs that? You toss the folded sheet behind you and back out of the box.

"Hey — where are the spacemen?" you mutter.

When you turn around, the robot is standing.

It got up on its own! So it *was* already on!

The huge toy walks forward, turns a corner — and heads straight for your room!

Follow the Annihilator to PAGE 95.

You can't grab the wheel. You don't even know how to drive!

Besides, Bobaloo seems to be slowing down. Bringing the car to a halt.

You peer through the window into the dark. You're in the woods somewhere. You can see that much. Miles and miles from any lights.

Even if you could scream, no one would hear you.

"Let's go," Bobaloo says, yanking open the back door. You step onto the soft ground. Strange animals rustle in the leaves.

Benny switches on a flashlight, lighting up a dirt path to a shack.

"Hurry up," Bobaloo urges, giving you a nudge.

You stumble along the path, with Bobaloo and Benny right behind. Bobaloo opens the shack door. Inside, you see nothing. Nothing except a dark hole in the ground.

Bobaloo pulls the sock out of your mouth. Then he removes the duct tape so you can use your hands.

"Climb down," Benny orders you, shining his light at the hole.

Do what Benny says on PAGE 106.

A jagged flash of lightning brightens the sky.

When it's gone, you notice the sky is a dark greenish gray. While you were putting out fires, a storm was moving in.

CRACCKKK! KA-BOOM!

Thunder!

It's right over the house. Then the wind and rain start. The storm is so loud and violent, it sounds like a freight train outside your door.

WHHHIRRRRR . . .

The Annihilator doesn't seem to care about the storm. It's still watching you. Standing guard. As if it's trying to keep you from leaving the kitchen. . . .

Every cell in your body is telling you to run for your life. To get out of the house. To run to your neighbor, Mrs. Carlyle.

But you're sure that if you leave, you'll never see your home again. The Annihilator will destroy it.

The red lights that serve as its eyes are dim, barely glowing. What is it thinking? *Can* it think?

You start to wonder if there's a way you could trick it.

If you try to trick the robot, turn to PAGE 51.
If you run to Mrs. Carlyle's house, turn to PAGE 97.

Your knees shake as Nasty Kathy marches you through the dim warehouse.

She takes you through a gray steel door in the warehouse. Then down a pitch-black staircase. You're frightened as you stumble down the steps in the dark. But you're even more frightened of the Laser Blaster in Nasty Kathy's hands.

At the bottom of the stairs, she pushes you through another door. From the glow on Nasty Kathy's Laser Blaster, you can see you're in a cement block basement room. It's like a dungeon.

"Try to ruin our plans from in here!" Nasty Kathy cackles. She slams the door — and locks you in the dark!

Turn to PAGE 29.

There's got to be some way to get the Annihilator back into its box, you decide.

But how? You stare at the box for a minute, racking your brain for a good idea.

WHHIRRR . . .

The robot is moving again. It walks over to its cardboard box. It flashes its lights.

Hey — what's it looking at? you wonder.

Then you see it. The spacemen! It's looking at a picture of the spacemen that were supposed to come with it in the box. That's what it's programmed to destroy.

You race to your little brother Geoffrey's room and dig around in his toy box. You know he's got an old plastic spaceman in there somewhere. It's his favorite toy.

Finally you find it. A red plastic space pilot. One of its arms is missing. But it will have to do.

You hurry back to the living room.

"Hey — robot!" you call. "Look what I have!"

The Annihilator lurches toward you. Its eyes light up and start flashing when it sees the spaceman in your hands.

Quickly you toss the spaceman into the cardboard box and stand back.

Turn to PAGE 16.

Instantly you know what those glowing eyes belong to. You've seen them on TV. They're horrible monster toys. Monsters called Zorgs.

On the toys, the claws are plastic and the teeth are rubber.

But, now, in the dim emergency light, you can see that these Zorgs are different — because they're alive.

Their claws and teeth are steel. Their mouths drip with green slime and purple ooze. Their eyes glow with a hideous green light.

You know what they want. Beyond any doubt. You saw the movie *Zorg Revenge* and you know what Zorgs do. They claw their way to your face — and rip it to shreds!

Zorgs swarm your face because it's the fastest way to get . . . to your brain!

The six Zorgs creep toward you. Their slimy feet make sucking noises as they grip and release the floor.

SQUISH. FLAP. SQUISH. FLAP.

You back up slowly. Watching them. Praying there aren't any more Zorgs behind you.

The six creatures sense your fear. They close in steadily.

Without warning, they all LEAP AT YOU!

Quick! Turn to PAGE 58.

"*What?*" you sputter. "*You're* a doll?"

Benny pulls off his shoe and shows you his foot. There, in his heel, you see a battery pack!

You're so amazed, you can't speak. You just stare at him.

"If you had put the key in IT'S TIM while I was still inside the factory, I would have died," Benny explains. "By the way, I'm the one who put your name on the list for the factory tour. I wanted you to see how cool the live toys were. I didn't realize how dangerous it would be. Nasty Kathy turned so mean!"

You open your mouth, but for a few seconds you can only manage a faint croak. Finally your voice works.

"Okay, so you're a toy. But what about this secret plan?" you ask him. "Why life-sized dolls?"

Benny gives you a small smile. "Oh, that's a story for another day," he tells you mysteriously.

He's right, of course. It's a story for another day — or another page. But for now, you're happy to know that you've had some fun — and came out of it alive in

THE END.

That sucking sound. It can mean only one thing.
The Zorgs are on your trail!

Frantically, you scan the shelves near you. Hunting for a Laser Blaster — or anything. Some kind of weapon so you can defend yourself against the face-rippers.

You fling aside boxes of video-game cartridges. There's lots of cool stuff you'd love to try out.

But you can't find a weapon!

The Zorgs scuttle forward, their green eyes glowing in the dark. They're close enough to leap. . . .

You can almost feel their claws ripping into you. And the stinging purple ooze from their tongues. . . .

In a panic, you grab the nearest thing — a package of walkie-talkies. You tear off the wrapping, stuff one walkie-talkie into the waistband of your jeans, and hurl the other at your friend.

"Benny! Catch!" you shout.

"I can't!" Benny cries.

Oops! You forgot. His hands are tied.

The walkie-talkie bounces off Benny's stomach and clatters into a corner.

The Zorgs are coming faster. You head for the doll aisle.

Hurry to PAGE 73 before the Zorgs get you. . . .

You turn around slowly. At first you don't see anyone. Then you glance down — and gasp.

At your feet on the floor are two small police officers. They're only a foot tall. But they look very tough.

Oh, no! you realize. You used a toy phone to call 911 — so they sent toy police!

The one who tapped you jerks his head toward a small police car. It's about the size of a shoe box.

"Get in," he orders. "You're under arrest for breaking and entering."

"Wait!" you cry. "You can't arrest me. I called you!"

The two cops glance at each other and laugh. "The kid says we can't make an arrest," the first cop says, and sneers.

"Ha," the second cop adds. "We'll see about that!"

The officers radio for backup. Soon, six more arrive. A moment later all eight tiny cops are pushing and shoving — forcing you into the backseat of the little squad car.

They accuse you of breaking and entering.

Now they're going to have to break *you* before you can enter that car!

Oh, well. Sometimes you just get a bad break.

THE END

You decide to take a chance on the front door. The toy policeman might be right on the other side. But facing just one of him beats being trapped in the building with Nasty Kathy and her army of terrible toys!

You race after Benny. The two of you crash through the front door of the factory. You stumble to a halt outside, trying to catch your breath.

"What *was* that?" Benny gasps as the factory door slams shut. "A bad dream?"

"Sssshhhh! Keep it down," you whisper. You glance around for any sign of the toy police officer.

The sky is turning dark. The parking lot is empty, except for one car. An old, rusty sedan parked in the corner. There are two people in the car. One has curly blond hair.

It's Bobaloo! The bum who just left you in that freaky factory by yourselves!

"Come on," you whisper to Benny, "let's find out what's really going on here!"

Sneak up to the car and listen on PAGE 100.

"Move out of the way!" Whittle yells at you.

Then he lunges at you. He grabs your arm. With a strong yank, he pulls you out of the line of fire.

ZAP! ZZZT. ZZRRTT. ZAP!

The new Annihilator sends out one laser beam after another — zapping the old robot!

Instantly, the old robot fires back.

You can't believe it. The two toys are battling it out in your living room.

"What's happening?" you scream.

Whittle doesn't answer. He just grips you tighter.

Turn to PAGE 49.

You get up and race after the robot.

"Hey! Wait!" you call.

You catch up with the Annihilator as it stalks into your room. "Hold on! Stop!" you cry out.

At the sound of your voice, the Annihilator whirls around and glares at you.

Its eyes light up, bright red. And then it grows silent. As if it's thinking. Even the *whirring* noises stop.

Somehow, the silence is creepy. *Very* creepy.

Cautiously, you step forward and reach your hand out to the robot. You've got to find the OFF switch.

The robot suddenly spins toward your bed. It raises its arm — and shoots out a laser beam. Whoa! Your bed is on fire!

What kind of toy is this?

Flames lap at the posters hanging over your bed.

You've got to do something! Your eyes dart around your room and land on your fish tank. Should you use the water to douse the flames? Or should you try to beat them out with your pillow?

Hurry — the fire's getting bigger!

If you go for the pillow, turn to PAGE 34.
If you grab the fish tank, turn to PAGE 52.

You have the silver key to Nasty Kathy's trunk. Ooooh. Too bad.

The silver key is nice. Very nice.

The problem with the silver key is that it only opens one thing.

Nasty Kathy's trunk!

You need a different key to survive this story.

Looks like you won't be turning off the toys anytime soon. . . .

Which is unfortunate. Because here come those Zorgs again!

SQUISH. FLAP. SQUISH. FLAP.

Uh-oh. It's going to get ugly this time.

The Zorgs are heading right for you.

Crawling up toward your face.

Nibbling your cheeks.

They're . . .

Stop! Close the book. This is too much!

Just face it —

This is

THE END!

Thunder crashes again and again. Lightning flickers every few seconds. Rain lashes the kitchen windows.

The storm is scary. But you're not staying here with that maniac robot. You've got to get out!

You glance at the back door. Then you sneak a quick look at the Annihilator.

Will it let you leave?

Or will it try to fry you when you make a run for it?

You take a few deep breaths and gather your courage.

Then you dart for the door, twist the handle, and . . .

EEEEEEEE! A piercing shriek blasts out of the robot.

It shoots a red laser at your hand. But it misses. Sparks jump from the door frame inches from your hand.

You swing the door open and run into the windy, rainy night!

You stumble and try to wipe the rain from your eyes. The wind is so strong, you can barely run against it.

A bright light flashes behind you!

The Annihilator! you think. You fall face first into the mud and wait for the laser blast to pierce your back.

Turn to PAGE 8.

There's no time to lose! Without thinking another second, you dash off to follow the doll.

You drop to your knees and crawl under a big piece of machinery. Then you snake your way through the factory, toward the big glass wall.

You see a glass door closing slowly. And a flash of pink.

The doll must have snuck into the warehouse.

"Benny!" you shout, running back to find him.

He's standing in front of a bank of video monitors with joysticks in both hands. Bobaloo is nowhere in sight.

"This is so cool!" Benny shouts. "Come on — try it!"

"Forget that," you answer. "I just saw a doll come to life! You've got to help me find it."

"Yeah, right." Benny smirks.

You grab the joysticks from him and toss them down.

"Come on," you answer. "I'll prove it."

Drag Benny to PAGE 20.

As you fall, you reach out and grab at the handle of a tennis racket on a dining room chair. You miss.

THWACK! The racket flips up. A tennis ball that was resting on the racket flies through the air.

The ball strikes the face of your mother's prize grandfather clock. The glass shatters.

When Patches hears the breaking glass, she screeches in fright. Then she runs from the corner where she was crouched. She races through the living room, into the dining room, and jumps onto a tall, tippy set of shelves by the wall.

Slowly, you shake yourself, trying to stand up.

You lift yourself to your knees.

And then . . .

WHHIRRR . . .

The Annihilator walks toward you . . .

Just as the tippy shelves begin to topple forward . . .

"Oh, no!" you cry as the bookshelves hurtle down.

Get out of the way on PAGE 108.

100

You and Benny duck down and crawl toward the car until you're within earshot.

"I had to take care of a glitch in the plan while I was giving those two kids the tour," Bobaloo is saying. "I told the brats to leave, but they didn't. Now we'll have to take care of them."

Uh-oh. Your skin begins to crawl.

Then you notice something even creepier. You nudge Benny. "Look!" you whisper. "Look at the other person in the car. It's that toy policeman, Officer Murphy!"

"What next?" the officer asks Bobaloo.

"Hike into town. Find the gas station on Main Street," Bobaloo says. "The owner is one of us. He'll give you a patrol car."

One of us? you think. Just what does that mean? Is Bobaloo a toy too?

Turn to PAGE 127.

You decide to trust Benny. You have to trust *someone*! This nightmare is too big to carry alone.

And, besides, you're the one who invited Benny to the toy factory. Not the other way around.

Of course, it never occurs to you that Benny might be the person — or the toy — who sent you the letter about winning the tour in the first place!

Fine. Live in a dream world if you want to.

But don't kid yourself. You have to wake up and face the real ending to this story one of these days!

Until then, enjoy your

HAPPY ENDING!

THWACK. KA-CHUNK! THWACK. KA-CHUNK!

You feel the machine poking holes in your new plastic scalp, and punching in new strands of hair.

You catch another glimpse of yourself in the mirror. Your mouth is curved into a permanent smile. Your red plastic lips are slightly open.

Yuck!

You're a doll! A dopey, smiling, life-sized doll.

Nasty Kathy strolls up to you as you sit there on the conveyor belt.

"So," she snarls. "Now you're one of us. Are you going to help us with our plan — or not?"

Well? What do you want to do?

If you agree to join Nasty Kathy's army, turn to PAGE 105.

If you don't want to help the toys, turn to PAGE 27.

"Get off me!" you cry, kicking your leg to shake the monster off.

But the thing is too strong. It won't let go.

It moves incredibly fast. Before you can even get a glimpse of it, it climbs your leg — then grasps your T-shirt. It scuttles toward your face.

You want to run — but you're frozen in panic.

"Listen to me," it says in your ear.

Huh? You crane your neck to see what it is.

It's a hand.

And nothing else!

A rubber bloody hand. Like you would buy at Halloween. It makes a fist on your shoulder and uses its thumb like a mouth.

"Listen to me," the hand warns. "That's the *wrong key*. Look inside her trunk for the right one."

Huh? How did the hand even know what you were searching for?

The Zorgs appear at the far end of the aisle — running this time. *SQUISH. FLAP-FLAP-FLAP! SQUISH!*

Better think fast. Can you trust a rubber bloody hand? Maybe this is a trap.

If you trust the hand, turn to PAGE 109.
If you think it's a trap, turn to PAGE 80.

Then Bobaloo flips on a light.

You gaze around. And gasp.

The Dark Hole is nothing like what you expected. It's not a dungeon. It's a big conference room! With charts on the walls. And maps. And a huge fancy oak table.

"This is our headquarters," Bobaloo says. "And we're prepared to tell you everything. But only if you promise not to tell anyone. Ever."

You nod silently. You're too surprised to speak.

"Let's show him," Bobaloo says, smiling at Benny.

Benny bends down and removes one shoe. He holds up his foot. There's a battery pack in the bottom!

"I *am* a toy," Benny admits. "My batteries are low. That's why I worried about riding my bike. Bobaloo is a toy too."

"I knew it!" you cry. "And Amy too? And my dad?"

"No, no," Benny goes on. "They're humans. They know nothing about us — or our plans."

"What plans?" you ask.

"We're on a mission," Benny replies. "The toys invented us so we could live in the town. Among humans. And change things."

"Ch-change *what*?" you stammer, gulping.

Hear the plan on PAGE 128.

"Okay," you tell Nasty Kathy. "I'll join you."

You don't think about it for more than a minute. What other choice do you have? You're a toy now.

Actually, you think, it's kind of cool being a doll! Your plastic body is tough. You'll never have to worry about mosquito bites again. Or sunburns.

And best of all, now you finally get to find out about the toys' mysterious plan!

"Welcome aboard," Nasty Kathy says, shaking your hand. "Okay, here's the deal. . . ."

Find out more on PAGE 56.

106

Now you can see that the hole isn't just a bottomless dirt pit. It's like a deep well. Made of cement. With a metal ladder running down one side.

Bobaloo motions for you to climb down.

"Go on," Benny says, and he leans toward you.

"Okay!" you cry. "Don't push me. I'll go!" You quickly climb down the ladder into the hole.

At the bottom, you find a cement floor — and a door. Benny and Bobaloo follow you down the ladder. Then Bobaloo unlocks the door and opens it.

"Get in," Bobaloo tells you, motioning for you to enter the dark room.

"Please don't lock me in," you beg. "Please."

Bobaloo shoves you into the cold, dark room. He and Benny step in behind you. You tremble in terror.

Now what?

Find out what's in the Dark Hole on PAGE 104.

You dash to Aisle One. You grab IT'S TIM and load your arms with other cool toys as well. Then you spot the pig — he's been following you up and down the aisles.

Why not? You tuck him under your arm. He grunts happily.

You snake around the edge of the warehouse and into the factory. You reach the front door.

"Hold it right there, you flesh freaks!" Nasty Kathy suddenly shouts over her megaphone.

You whip around. YIKES! She's right behind you! And the Laser Blaster is pointed at your face!

Without hesitating, Benny tosses a hockey stick at Nasty Kathy. She ducks out of the way. Giving you just enough time to slip out of the factory and slam the door shut.

"We did it!" you cry.

"Get back here, humans!" Nasty Kathy shouts from inside.

Benny grabs IT'S TIM from you.

"Where's the key?" he asks impatiently.

You hand him the computer disk, feeling confused. He shoves it into a slot in the back of the Talking Speller.

Instantly, there is a flash of blinding white light. Then a loud hum that fades into silence.

Find out what happened on PAGE 132.

You gasp. Then you cover your head and desperately roll out of the way.

The bookshelves crash to the floor, crushing everything in their path.

Including the Annihilator!

When the crash is over, the toy lies in a twisted, broken heap under the bookshelves. One arm has slid across the floor. The rest of the Annihilator is buried under the weight of two hundred books.

You get to your feet, still shaking, just as your mom walks in the back door with your little brother.

She takes one look at the mess and gasps.

"I can't believe it!" she cries. "This place looks like a war zone. What happened? How did you do it?"

For a minute, you consider telling her the truth. About the evil Annihilator that was after you. . . .

Then you realize that she'll never, ever believe you.

"How did I do it?" you ask with a silly grin. "Just clumsy, I guess!"

THE END

The Zorgs are closing in. *SQUISH! FLAP!*

Every nerve in your body screams: RUUUN!

But something tells you that the bloody hand is telling the truth.

"Find the real key," it says with its thumb. "When you find it, put it in the Incredible Talking Spelling Thinking Intelligent Machine."

"The *what?*" you demand.

The creature lets go and falls off your shoulder. With its bloody fingers spread out, it looks like a giant red spider.

"*Aaahhhhh!*" it screams all the way down to the floor.

"Thanks for the hand," you call. "Uh — I mean, thanks for the advice."

Quickly, you unlock Nasty Kathy's trunk and peer inside.

Dirty, torn doll clothes. An archery set. A miniature can of spray paint . . .

Then you spot a small computer diskette. It's like the cartridges that came with your little brother's Talking Speller.

You grab the disk and hold it under the light.

There's a picture of a key on it.

BINGO!

Snatch the key and race to PAGE 65.

110

You pick up your dad's laptop computer and hand it over to the Annihilator. You don't want to do it. But you're terrified of what the robot might do to you if you refuse.

Then you close your eyes and put your fingers in your ears. You don't want to watch the Annihilator smash the expensive computer to bits.

You wait for the horrible smash.

Silence. Nothing.

Huh? What's going on?

Finally you can't stand the suspense. You open your eyes.

You can't quite believe what you see.

The robot is sitting at your dad's desk with the computer open in front of it.

And it's typing!

Go to PAGE 72.

Benny's left shoe is off. You stare at his foot in horror.

In the heel is a battery compartment. Just like the compartment in the police doll's foot.

Suddenly you understand why Benny didn't want you to put the key in IT'S TIM. He knew that if you turned off the toys, you'd turn him off too. Because he wasn't really alive.

He was running on batteries.

Benny is a doll too!

"I'm sorry," you say to Benny, standing over him sadly.

Then you realize something.

You're talking to a doll!

You feel bad about Benny. But after all, you hadn't known him very long. And you did always think he was kind of weird.

Oh, well, you think as you walk out of the factory. At least you didn't get zapped by Nasty Kathy.

You start to pedal your bike home. But suddenly you're hit with a horrible thought.

If Benny was a doll — who else is a toy too?

Your father? Your mother? Your best friend?

Guess you'd better start reading again. Until you find out the answer to that, you haven't really come to

THE END. . . .

112

Benny climbs into the front seat with Bobaloo. The car pulls back onto the road.

You yank on the car door handles. But they're locked. They won't open from the inside.

"Why are you doing this, Benny?" you cry.

"Put a sock in it," Bobaloo commands over his shoulder.

Benny bends over and starts untying his shoelaces. A moment later, he whirls around. He leans into the backseat and stuffs his sock in your mouth.

Oh, gross! You want to scream. But you can't make a sound. Not with Benny's dirty, smelly sock in your mouth.

You strain to see the bottom of his feet, but they're hidden by the seat. You reach up to remove the sock. But Benny grabs your wrists and lashes them together with duct tape.

The truth hits you. You're not going to get out of this. They'll stick you in the Dark Hole — and never let you out!

You're desperate, but you can't think of anything to do. Except lean over the seat and grab the steering wheel.

The trouble is, with your hands taped, you aren't sure you could control the car. It could be very dangerous!

If you grab the wheel, turn to PAGE 21.
If you think grabbing the wheel is too risky, go to PAGE 85.

You stand still and try to listen. But your heart is pounding so loudly, it's all you can hear.

Then a noise comes from down the hall. A noise that makes the back of your neck prickle.

"Meeeooooww!"

It's Patches, your cat! She's in trouble. And you think you know what's causing it.

Please, you think, let Patches be okay!

Find out if Patches is okay on PAGE 46.

THWACK. KA-CHUNK. THWACK...

You squeeze your eyes shut. Any second now, mechanical arms are going to swoop down, poke holes in your head, and stuff it full of doll hair!

Then, suddenly, something incredible happens.

A voice comes out of the walkie-talkie in the waistband of your jeans. It's muffled, but everyone can hear it.

"Don't hurt me," a small, high-pitched voice says. "Please believe me. I'm a toy!"

That voice. You recognize it.

It's the pig!

The head ninja runs over to the switch and stops the hair-planting machine. "The voice came out of its stomach!" the ninja cries. "A human can't do that!"

"It *must* be a toy!" another ninja shouts.

"Of course I'm a toy," the pig's voice answers. "Let me go!"

The pig must have found the other walkie-talkie near Benny!

Silently, you promise never to eat another slice of bacon as long as you live.

Three ninjas jump onto the conveyor belt.

And bring their swords flashing down at your head!

Go to PAGE 136.

You and Benny slip around to the back of the car. You lift the trunk lid slightly and squeeze in.

Seconds later, Bobaloo pulls away.

"We did it!" Benny whispers triumphantly.

"We're nuts," you answer.

You know you shouldn't be riding in the trunk of a stranger's car. Especially a stranger who probably isn't even human! You're terrified of what will happen if Bobaloo catches you.

But you *must* find out what he's up to.

You grip the trunk lid tightly so it won't bounce around or slam shut.

Finally, Bobaloo pulls to a stop. When you hear him get out of the car, you lift the trunk lid and take a peek.

"I see a small airplane. Bobaloo is getting on board!" you tell Benny.

"I've always wanted to stow away on a plane," Benny says.

Can that be a good idea? you think.

Definitely not.

Do it, anyway, on PAGE 57.

You can't take your eyes off the Laser Blaster. It looks so big. The red and blue lights on its barrel flash on and off. On and off. It's just a toy, you tell yourself. A plastic toy.

But toys have a way of being dangerous around here.

What if that Laser Blaster is alive too? It could blow you to bits. . . .

"Well, look who it is!" Nasty Kathy sneers. "Dorky Porky and his new friend — the pile of human guts."

You swallow hard. The truth is, Nasty Kathy is terrifying. She's only two feet tall — but she looks so evil, it makes her seem bigger somehow.

"Oooink!" the pig squeals, and trots off.

"I'll see *you* later, fatso," Nasty Kathy calls. "As for you, let's go. On your feet, human!"

She jerks the Laser Blaster in the direction she wants you to walk.

Do you dare make a run for it?

If you dare to make a run for it, turn to PAGE 53.

If you think you'd better do what she says, turn to PAGE 87.

Whittle lifts the new robot out of its box and sends it striding toward your house.

The new Annihilator clomps up your front steps. At the front door, it stops and waits. A moment later, Whittle leaps onto your porch.

"Let me in!" he yells, pounding on the door with his fists.

"No! Go away!" you shout.

Whittle peers in through the front window at you and scowls.

"I'm coming in," he announces in a gruff voice. "And you can't stop me!"

WHIRRR . . .

Oh, no. That sound . . .

You don't dare turn around. But you know what's happening. The Annihilator — the one that's already in your house — has walked into the living room. It's standing right behind you.

You can't move.

You can't leave.

You're trapped!

Turn to PAGE 30.

118

A small stuffed pig peers down at you. And blinks.

"It's true," the pig says. "She *is* alive. I am too!"

You and Benny gasp. The fuzzy pink pig is squirming to get out of the twist-tie holding it inside its package.

You both start to back away.

"Pleeeease wait," squeals the pig. "Please help me out of my box. Every night I have to get out by myself, and it's h-h-hard."

You look up and see that the pig has a tear in one eye. It's crying!

As you reach up to help the pig, you hear something. A rustling noise, like water, or wind. It seems to be coming from all around you. . . .

Out of the corner of your eye, you see movement. Something just flitted across the aisle!

Then it dawns on you. The rustling noise? It's paper. And cardboard. And plastic. And right now, every single toy in the warehouse is doing something incredible. Something you thought only happened in a kid's best dream — or worst nightmare.

Thousands of toys: *all* coming to life.

Turn to PAGE 24.

Your heart hammers as you dash into the night. Before you know it, you're at your house. You run around to the back door.

As you're turning the knob, you peer through the glass in the door. Your dad is seated on a kitchen stool with his back to you.

He has one foot propped on the opposite knee — and his shoe is off. He's doing something to his foot!

You flash back in the factory — you can still see that plastic ninja toy dropping batteries into the policeman's heel.

Is it possible that your own dad is a life-sized toy?

Who can you trust? Where can you go that's safe?

You turn and run again. Blindly. Not knowing where to go.

But as you race through the night, you suddenly realize you're heading for your best friend's house. Amy's. You've got to see her. She's the one person you know you can trust.

You ring her doorbell. Panting. Out of breath.

The door swings open. But it's not Amy who's standing there. It's someone else. The last person you expected to see. . . .

Find out who it is on PAGE 83.

You won't give up without a fight.

You jump up. "Your plan is going to fail, Bobaloo!" you shout at him. "And you're not putting us in the Dark Hole!"

Bobaloo's face starts to twitch. Soon he's grinning. Then he's laughing. The two goons behind him laugh too.

"You have spunk, kid," Bobaloo says. "I like that! I'm going to give you a reward."

He gestures to the goons. They pull a lever, and a door slides open. Cold wind blasts into the plane.

"Guess what your reward is," Bobaloo says.

"We're going to Walt Disney World?" Benny asks hopefully.

"No!" Bobaloo laughs again. "Your reward is . . . *skydiving lessons!*"

Uh-oh.

"I never went skydiving before," you say. "I don't even know how to use a parachute."

"We'll make it easy, then," Bobaloo says. "For this first jump, we won't use any parachutes."

Easy? Not quite.

Looks as if you're going to learn the *hard* way!

THE END

You've got the computer disk in your pocket. The one you found inside Nasty Kathy's trunk.

And you remember where the rubber hand told you to put it. In the Incredible Talking Spelling Thinking Intelligent Machine.

Your heart pounds as you race down the aisle.

Frantically, your eyes scan every box, every toy on the shelf. Puzzles. Reading games. Math machines. Mazes. Alphabet games.

Everything but a Talking Speller!

"Where is it?" you cry out in frustration.

The pig's voice suddenly bursts out of the walkie-talkie in your waistband. "IT'S TIM!" the pig yells.

Huh? It's Tim?

Who's Tim?

Turn to PAGE 129.

It's Patches! She's dragging an ice cube on the end of her tail. The Annihilator must have zapped her with its freeze-beam!

Patches *meows* unhappily and twitches her tail, trying to shake the ice off.

The Annihilator strides in behind her and stops. Its eyes glow. It seems to be staring straight at you.

Patches darts behind your legs and cowers there.

The Annihilator just stands there. Not moving.

Somehow, that makes you more scared. Not less. It's as if the robot is thinking . . . planning . . .

Plotting what to do next.

The hair on the back of your neck stands up.

I'll call 911, you think.

But as you reach for the phone, a horrible high-pitched noise blares out of the Annihilator's head: *SCREEEEEEEEECH!*

A quick burst of laser beam shoots from its hand. A bright red line of light zaps straight into the wall phone.

ZZZZTT!

Slowly you pick up the receiver. You bring it to your ear.

No dial tone. The line is dead!

Don't make any sudden moves. Just put the phone down and turn to PAGE 66.

"No, Benny!" you shout. "Let's find a different way out."

You dash away, through the twisting aisles of the warehouse. You don't dare slow down to peek over your shoulder. All you can do is hope Benny is following you.

Nasty Kathy's voice booms over her megaphone.

"Alert!" she shouts. "A ball of human fungus is loose in our warehouse. If it escapes, I'll have you all taken apart!"

The second she finishes speaking, you hear the whir of toy motors and the clatter of plastic feet.

You keep running, even though your lungs are about to burst. You need to find cover! Then you see that you've run right into the main aisle. And you realize you've made a mistake.

A terrible mistake.

It sounds as if the entire warehouse full of toys is coming for you! Surrounding you!

Then you see six pairs of eyes — glowing green eyes — closing in. . . .

"No!" you scream.

Meet your fate on PAGE 89.

"Heeeeeelp!" You kick and scream, struggling to get free.

In a burst of strength, you break your arms and legs out of the sticky web!

But it's too late. Two huge mechanical arms move in to hold you in place. A large, flat panel slides under your back, then bends, forcing you to sit up. A bowl-shaped thing whirs into place over your head.

You squint your eyes and grit your teeth. Any minute now the hole-punching should begin. . . .

Then you catch your reflection in the shiny machine.

Hey! The bowl-shaped thing above you is a giant plastic doll scalp! You watch, horrified, as the machine lowers it onto your head. Then it fits a plastic doll's face over yours, molding it into place! You can see through the eye slits.

The machine molds plastic arms and legs around your own. Soon you're covered in plastic.

They're turning you into a life-sized doll!

Turn to PAGE 102.

You're saying you stopped in Aisle Three and picked up a handheld video game?

Who do you think you're kidding?

You didn't stop in Aisle Three at all!

You didn't pick up a video game.

This book is the only game you played. And guess what?

YOU LOSE!

GAME OVER

126

"You're lying," you say to Benny, staring him right in the eye. "I don't trust you for a second. In fact, I don't trust anyone anymore! Maybe you're all toys! Even you, Amy. Maybe even my mom and dad are toys!"

Amy opens her mouth to argue, but you won't listen.

"I'm calling the government!" you shout as you dart away from your friends and out the door.

You run into the night. An owl hoots in the trees. From the other end of town you hear a police siren. You keep running. There's a pay phone at the end of your block. You're going to call the FBI!

You lift the receiver and dial "O" for the operator.

Just then a car pulls up next to the phone booth. A rusty old sedan.

The phone is ringing now on the other end. Pick up! you think. Please pick up!

But it's already too late. You feel a hand reaching over your shoulder.

Find out whose hand that is on PAGE 135!

"What about the two kids?" Officer Murphy asks.

"Spread the word," Bobaloo says. "Tell the others to be on the watch for them. Once we catch them, we may have to take them to the Dark Hole."

"The Dark Hole?" Murphy says. Then you hear an eerie sound, like an alarm clock getting smashed over and over with a sledgehammer.

Yikes! The toy policeman is . . . laughing.

Turn to PAGE 13.

Change things? What do the toys want to change?

"Everything," Benny answers. "We're going to change the laws so kids have more time off from school. And we'll give kids video games instead of schoolbooks. And change school lunches too. More pizza. Less broccoli. Get it? But it takes a lot of adults to vote for stuff like that. That's why we need mostly toys that look like grownups."

As Benny talks, Bobaloo shows you pictures of the plan. Kids on new bikes grin happily. Kids wave from awesome rides installed in a school playground. Kids laugh as they cram cotton candy into their mouths in a cafeteria.

Cool. It's a plot to make the world more fun for kids!

Benny puts his hand on your shoulder. "Bobaloo and I decided to tell you about the plan because we've got a very important job for you. You're going to be in charge!"

In charge? Sounds great!

That is, until you find out what "in charge" really means.

All the toys run on — what else? — batteries. And guess who gets to keep all those batteries charged up?

That's right. *You.* You just keep going . . . and going . . . and going . . .

THE END

You don't get it. Why is the pig yelling about someone named Tim?

Then you catch sight of it. And it all makes sense.

Incredible Talking Spelling Thinking Intelligent Machine.

A red plastic toy, shaped like a book. And the first letter of each word spells out IT'S TIM!

You are about to insert the disk — when you hear Benny's voice. From two aisles over. He sounds terrified.

"Don't do it!" he cries. "Whatever you do, don't put the key in IT'S TIM!"

How does Benny know what you're doing? Did he figure it out from the soldiers? Does he know something you don't know?

He's your friend. Should you listen to him?

If you do, you might miss your chance to turn off the toys. You can hear Nasty Kathy's voice nearby. She's coming. She must have heard the pig yell, "It's Tim!"

And if she catches you, this time you might not get away!

"Please! Don't!" Benny cries. "If only you knew —"

Well?

If you put the key in IT'S TIM, turn to PAGE 43.

If you want to find out what Benny knows, run over to PAGE 68.

130

Parked at the curb is a shiny black car with dark tinted windows. The words HASLEY TOY COMPANY are printed on the side.

As the rain pours down a tall, thin man gets out and opens the trunk. That's Whittle, you think. It's got to be!

Whittle is the scariest-looking person you've ever seen. A hideous six-inch-long scar slashes across his left cheek. His stringy black hair blows wildly in the wind. His eyes are like black marbles: hard, shiny, and cold. He's wearing a black leather jacket and black leather gloves.

Something about the way he opens and closes his gloved fists makes you want to run screaming for help.

Instead, you run to the front door and double-bolt the lock. Then you peer out through the curtains. Whittle is lifting a large box out of the trunk of his car.

No! You want to scream when you see what's in the box.

It's *another* Annihilator!

Turn to PAGE 117.

Benny runs toward you.

"Those ninjas caught me when I was trying to run out. They had me surrounded!" he pants. "I thought I was dead! And then they were just — gone!" He snaps his fingers.

"Where did everything go?" you ask, your mouth hanging open so wide, you could probably fit Nasty Kathy's head in there.

"The toys? Oh, that was all a hologram," Bobaloo explains. "This is a new theme park called TOY WORLD. The whole thing is done with holograms. From that box there." He points at the gray box.

Bobaloo explains that they're testing TOY WORLD to see if kids like it. And to see if it's scary enough.

"That's so cool!" you announce. "Can we come again?"

"Uh, sure," Bobaloo answers. "Here are some tickets."

He hands you a ticket book that says *Win Ten Tickets to Toy World!*

But when you read the small print, you see you haven't really won at all.

First you have to buy ten magazine subscriptions!

Happy reading!

THE END

You stare at Benny with wide eyes.

"What just happened?" you ask slowly.

"The toys went back to being just toys," he explains. "At least all the ones *inside* the factory."

"Huh?" you ask stupidly, your mouth hanging open.

"The toys we brought out are still alive," he goes on. "That's why I didn't want you to put the key in IT'S TIM until we got out. I knew that every toy — and every life-sized doll — in the factory would go to sleep forever when you used the key."

You blink. "I don't get it," you say. "You cared that much about keeping these toys alive?"

The pig under your arm squirms happily. "I'm glad you did, though," you add, giving the pig an affectionate squeeze.

"The toys are cool." Benny hesitates for a second. "But mostly I cared about keeping *myself* alive!"

"Keeping *yourself* alive?" you say. "What do you mean?"

Benny gazes solemnly at you.

"I'm going to tell you the truth," he says. "I knew all about the living toys. And that they were making human-looking dolls to carry out a secret plan. Because I'm a doll!"

Go on to PAGE 90.

Desperately, you glance at the red light again.

It's a beam of some sort, coming from a box in the corner of the wall.

What's it for? you wonder.

On instinct, you put the palm of your hand up, intercepting the beam.

The instant you do, all the toys in the warehouse . . . vanish!

They just . . . disappear. Every single one of them. Every game, car, doll, puzzle, and weapon.

Simply gone!

A second later, the bright overhead lights come on. Bobaloo bursts into the warehouse through the glass door.

"Okay, the tour's over," Bobaloo says cheerily. "How did you like it?"

Give him an answer on PAGE 131.

134

"Wait!" you cry out, kicking and squirming inside the spiderweb. "Wait! Let me go — please! I'll make it worth your while."

The army captain strokes his chin.

"Really?" he asks, sounding interested.

"Sure," you answer eagerly. "Anything! I'll give you anything. What do you want?"

"What have you got?" the captain asks.

Hmmm. Good question. What *have* you got?

"How about my old toys and games?" you offer weakly.

"Games? Toys? Are you kidding?! Ha!" The captain sweeps his arm toward the overflowing warehouse.

All the soldiers start laughing and slapping their knees. Even the ninjas chuckle.

"Turn on the machines!" the captain commands with a little wave of his hand.

"Wait! How about a bag of chocolate gold coins? A million dollars in Monopoly money?" you try.

But it's no use. The conveyor belt is moving again. You ride closer and closer to the hole-punching machine.

THWACK. KA-CHUNK!

Go to PAGE 124.

The hand grabs the phone and slams it down before anyone answers.

You turn around — and gasp.

Benny is standing there. And Bobaloo too!

Your jaw drops. So it's true. Benny *is* in on the toys' plot. That rat!

You want to scream for help, but your voice seems stuck.

"Let's go," Bobaloo says, grabbing your elbow roughly. "It's time to put an end to all of this."

You glance at Benny pleadingly. How could he do this? Even if he *is* a toy . . . he was your friend!

"Where to?" he asks Bobaloo. They both shove you into the backseat of the long black car.

"There's only one place," Bobaloo answers. *"The Dark Hole."*

Face the Dark Hole on PAGE 112.

You stare in horror at the flashing swords.

They sweep down on you . . .

And slice away the Instant Spiderweb that's tying you down!

A few seconds later, you're free.

You hop off the conveyor belt and open your mouth to say, "Thanks." But just then your walkie-talkie crackles to life again.

"Thank you for helping me," the voice in the walkie-talkie declares. "And now if you'll excuse me, I've got something important to do. In the warehouse — Aisle One."

"Sorry about that," the army captain mutters. "We were just following orders."

"You should think before you follow orders," the pig scolds through the walkie-talkie.

You smile to yourself as you hurry toward the glass wall. Then in through the glass door. Toward Aisle One.

Inside the door, you see Benny on the floor, still tied up with jump ropes. Right where the soldiers left him.

Only he's just lying there, curled up. Completely still.

Is he even breathing?

"Benny!" you call out. "Benny!"

Turn to PAGE 35.

The Annihilator looks confused for a moment.

Then it raises the truck above its head and smashes it down! Bright red pieces of plastic scatter all over the kitchen floor.

"Oh, no," you moan, backing up fearfully.

The Annihilator stalks toward you, its face lights flashing. Then it holds out one hand.

"What do you want?" you whisper. "Another toy to destroy?"

You glance around quickly. There — on the counter. Your little brother's plastic stretchy man. A toy called Big Bob.

Without getting too close, you push Big Bob toward the Annihilator.

The robot's lights flash eagerly as it picks up Big Bob. But the stretchy toy doesn't beep or glow.

The Annihilator doesn't like it!

With one powerful twist of its hands, it tears Big Bob's head off and slams it to the floor!

WHHIRRR...

The Annihilator gazes around again. For something else...

Hurry to PAGE 36 — before it tears your head off!

About R.L. Stine

R.L. Stine is the most popular author in America. He is the creator of the *Goosebumps*, *Give Yourself Goosebumps*, *Fear Street*, and *Ghosts of Fear Street* series, among other popular books. He has written more than 100 scary novels for kids. Bob lives in New York City with his wife, Jane, teenage son, Matt, and dog, Nadine.